The Dropout

Other Books by Jeffrey Zygmont

FICTION:

I Am Bill Gates' Dog

Ad Man in the Games of 2046

NON-FICTION:

Microchip
An Idea, Its Genesis and the
Revolution It Created

The VC Way
Investment Secrets from the
Wizards of Venture Capital

www.jeffreyzygmont.com

The Dropout

JEFFREY ZYGMONT

The Dropout

Copyright © 2013 by Jeffrey Zygmont

ISBN: 978-0-9838131-4-9 (Paperback)
ISBN: 978-0-9838131-5-6 (eBook)
LCCN: 2012954600

Publisher's Note: This is a work of fiction.
Names, characters, places and incidents either are the product of the
author's imagination or are used fictitiously, and any resemblance to
actual persons, living or dead, business establishments, products,
events or locales is entirely coincidental.

Free People Publishing
Salem, NH

Text layout and design by
Nancy Grossman

Cover design by Jeffrey Zygmont
Printed in the United States of America

for
Waldemar and Lucille Camann
Requiescat in Pace

T *he Dropout* was originally published in 2000 by a pioneering British book company called Online Originals. David Gettman, founder and chief editor at the time, started Online Originals with the revolutionary notion that books could be published electronically, to be read on computers. Unfortunately, his idea was about a decade ahead of history, before special-purpose computers called e-readers had been invented, and well before the e-books we know today became so commonplace. Online Originals did not survive as a literary venture that judiciously selects original works, and actually pays the authors who write them.

Nevertheless, I remain very grateful to David Gettman and his first-in-the-world e-book company, Online Originals, for publishing *The Dropout* at a time when I was still new to the book-writing vocation.

I revised *The Dropout* a dozen years later to re-issue it under my own imprint, Free People Publishing. Completed in 2012, the revision retains all of *The Dropout*'s original features, including references to products and technologies now out of date. But descriptions of a Ford LTD, a lumbering sedan you don't find even in used-car listings anymore, and depictions of people with calling cards visiting telephone booths, do not compromise the story or cloud its telling.

The Dropout was inspired by my wife's parents, Waldemar and Lucille Camann. I wrote the book after watching Lucille degenerate from Alzheimer's disease and Wally lose sense and composure because of his wife's demise. But fortunately for me, by then their life's work was well done, and I would forevermore have for my love their daughter Donna. With this little tale I thank them.

CHAPTER ONE

When I was nineteen years old and home for the summer after my first year of college, my father came home unexpectedly one afternoon and found me in bed with a woman named Linda.

Linda was an acquaintance from high school. Well, I couldn't even call her an acquaintance, really, because before that afternoon I don't think the two of us had ever exchanged a word. We came from two radically different crowds, and social circles among adolescents are as exclusionary as any ever get—unless you count people with money. In high school I had been one of the anointed: an athlete and honor student who was marked off as college bound. Linda belonged to the opposite set, the unruly kids who lived lives as close to an adult life as anyone who's fourteen or sixteen or eighteen can live, because they didn't get the coddling and sheltering from parents that the rest of us got, because their parents, presumably, were out living lives of childish irresponsibility themselves, too preoccupied or maybe just too selfish to pay much attention to their kids. Though I don't mean to suggest that we coddled kids were better off, necessarily. The point is, with Linda's background it was only natural for her to think that she and I could pass the afternoon undisturbed in my parents' house. But, come to think of it, it was only natural for me, the college boy, to expect that too, because by rights both my father and my mother should have stayed at work at least until supper time.

The encounter began quite by accident, when Linda and I bumped into each other at a little roadside park not far from my home. I had felt bored enough that afternoon to actually venture out for a walk, to see what mischief the world was stirring up. I'd been out for only a few minutes, kicking stones, scuffing my feet in the gravel beside the road, cutting through the little park on my way to no place in particular when I looked up suddenly and saw Linda. She appeared like a Delphic vision, sitting at a picnic table dead ahead of me, watching me, probably wondering if I was going to crash into her. Just a few more steps and I would have crashed into her. I hadn't noticed her there. I hadn't even noticed the table or even realized that someone else was in the park. There were no cars in the lot, and the place was almost always deserted anyway. It wasn't even a full-fledged park, really, just a little turn-off from a backwater country highway, a kind of grassy rest stop with a few picnic tables that survived from the days when the road actually led somewhere.

Yet here sat Linda. I stopped short and blurted out the word hello, more a startled reflex than a legitimate greeting. Linda looked amused by my surprise.

"Hello to you," she said, and I was relieved to hear only

good humor in her voice, instead of the chiding mockery I had unaccountably expected from her.

"I almost didn't see you," I went on.

"I know. Where you goin' in such a big hurry?"

"No place, really. I mean, I'm just out taking a walk."

"Well you really ought to watch where you're walkin' to," she joked. "For a second there I thought you were gonna run me down."

"I didn't think anyone else was here. I mean, I come here all the time and there's never anyone here. I live just over there."

"You live here? Really? I didn't know you lived near here."

"Yeah. In that white house. See. You can see it just over there."

"Damn," she said, "that's really a big house."

"It's pretty old. I'm supposed to help my father paint it this summer."

"Really?"

"Yeah."

"I never would of took you for the type that paints houses."

"I'm not. I mean, I've never painted one before. I'm only doing it because my father asked me to. I think he just wants us to do something together. You know: father and son."

We went on like that for a little while, stabbing at conversation. Linda, like me, seemed to have nothing better to do that afternoon. She'd come to the park originally to meet someone. At least that's what I assumed, because she seemed to be expecting an arrival. The few times a car approached on the highway she looked up at it expectantly. Her eyes followed it as far as the little siding where it would have to turn off to come into the park. None did. After a while she gave up looking. When our conversation ground down to where the intervals of silence were growing longer than the intervals of empty speech, when I realized that we were both staring down at her bare feet as though they were objects of great interest (although to me they really were objects of great interest), I asked her if she wanted to walk over to my house for something to drink, a cola or some juice or maybe just a glass of water, "because it's so hot out here today,""I said. "My parents have this new refrigerator that makes its own ice and dumps it right into your glass."I elaborated: "There's nobody home, so it's not like you have to meet anyone or anything."

The boldness of the invitation surprised me. At least it seemed bold to me. I was naive about the mysteries of courtship and seduction then. I hope that I'm naive about them still, because a person needs some innocence and ignorance to feel the full delight of life's surprises. In the park I simply could not tell if any sparks had struck between Linda and me, but I was desperately hoping that they had, and I realized that, for anything more to happen, we needed to get away to a secure and secluded, private nest that would screen us from distractions and intrusions. The knowledge came from instinct, I suppose. Whatever its source, when Linda accepted my offer I felt boastfully proud of my inventiveness: offering her a cold drink as a pretense for getting her alone. I thought it was brilliant, a line out of the book of a fabled lover. As I led her to the house I swelled with the hubris of a petty conqueror. A cold drink! I talked on about the new refrigerator, while Linda, smiling and eager to match my rapid pace, responded only occasionally with an "oh" and an "uh-huh" and a "really."

While I'm speaking true confessions, I should also admit that, for a young and eager post-adolescent with a deep summer's tan and a year's worth of experience in a college dorm, I made quite a mess of sex that afternoon. Probably I was too preoccupied by the secret knowledge that this was my first time, and, not wanting it to appear like my first time to Linda, I tried too hard to swagger too much. Maybe I'm the type who's just too preoccupied in general. Whatever the reason, I didn't give myself wholly to her. My mind remained detached, thoughtful and observant, while my body, I was surprised and pleased to discover, performed the rituals it was programmed to perform without any instructions from my intellect.

So at least it was halfway satisfying, which isn't bad, because a lot of time that's the most that anyone can say about sex anyway. And we were still only about halfway through. It might have gotten much better. But suddenly, without really seeing anything I became dimly aware of another presence in the room with us. Probably I heard him. Maybe I smelled him. Turning my head I saw him there, my father, framed by my bedroom doorway and looking in from the hall.

He disappeared instantly. I rolled off of Linda, bounded upward from the bed and landed with my feet on the floor in one acrobatic leap. I pulled on my shorts, tugged my shirt over my head and then rummaged frantically for my sneakers on the floor. Scooping them up with both hands I raced for the doorway. I raced to get out of there. Then suddenly I stopped, caught in mid-flight by the nag of a thought that had found its way out through my panic: what about Linda? Turning around I saw her there, still on the bed. Once again my mind detached itself, and in that brief instant of hesitation I noticed three things about the woman. First, she was beautiful. Second, I noticed that she was aroused. I hadn't expected that. Or rather, the possibility that I would excite her had simply never occurred to me. I'd been so preoccupied, I suppose, with my own performance and with keeping up my own image that the idea that my partner also had to be either feeling something or faking something hadn't entered my mind. In effect, I had been masturbating.

The third thing I realized about Linda was that she had no idea that my father was in the house. She watched me from the bed, propped up on an elbow, faint tan lines from a bathing suit outlining her nudity. She breathed in deeply, stretched out an arm as if to pull me gently back to her if she could only reach me. She smiled. "Where you goin'," she said. "I'm not through with you yet."

What could I possibly say to her? The panic blasted back into my head. My father was just down the hall now. In his own room. I could hear him there. What could I possibly say to her? I turned, sprinted the length of the hall, flew down the stairs and burst out the front door. I ran a ways down the road—going in the direction opposite the park—before I even stopped to slip on my sneakers.

I walked for hours before daring to return home. It was well past supper time then. The sun was hunkered down low on the horizon, that moment when the big shimmering disk looks like it's resting on the edge of the earth. When I walked into the house my mother called out that she'd left a plate of food in the refrigerator for me. I strained to detect in her voice any signs of disapproval, any signs that she knew anything at all, signs that my father had told her. The fact that she was talking at all, that she'd put up some dinner for me were both good signs. Upstairs I sat silently on my bed through a long, long stretch of torturous time, listening for any activity below, wondering whenever I heard their voices muffled above the noise from the TV if they were talking about me, cringing at the expectation, each time I heard footsteps, that my father might be coming right now to accost me.

But he didn't come. Confrontation wasn't in his nature. Not that he was particularly peaceable. I think he simply wanted to spare himself the anguish of conflict, so he overlooked a lot, ignored a lot, sacrificed intimacy for the sake of his comfort. I felt infinitely thankful for it that evening. Late into the night, after nothing had happened, I began to accept that I was in the clear. At least I'd be spared an embarrassing confrontation with my father and mother. I began to believe that I might even fall asleep. I almost did. But just as my thoughts grew scattered and distant and jumbled, just as a formless, comforting cloud of forgetfulness hazed over my brain, a second panic shook me awake again: I had no idea how Linda had made it out of the house. Maybe she had simply gathered up her clothing and left quietly, never discovering that my father had come home. Or maybe she hadn't heard me go out. Maybe she thought I was still in the house and maybe she had gone looking for me, poking playfully from room to room until she smacked up against him. Or maybe he returned to my room before she could make it out. What would they have said to each other?

As badly as I needed to know how Linda had escaped, there was no way to find out. I certainly couldn't ask my dad. And the last thing I wanted to do was look up Linda to ask her. She would mock me, I was sure. And even if she didn't, I would feel too humiliated to face her. I had deserted her. I had fled in a childish fright and no amount of swaggering could erase that. For a man-boy nothing can be more embarrassing than sexual cowardice. The only remedy was to avoid her. I spent the balance of that summer looking over my shoulder out of fear that I might run into Linda again. I couldn't leave the house without the trembling suspicion that she would pop up unexpectedly out there. I would round a street corner and there she would stand, laughing, pointing, telling the tale to all my friends, who would laugh too, and taunt me about how I had run out on her.

For that matter, I couldn't remain quite comfortable at home, either. I held my breath every time I heard my father approach, afraid that this might be the time that he was coming to demand an explanation. He never did. In fact, he seemed to avoid talking with me, just as I avoided talking with him, because there just didn't seem to be a way that we could talk about anything without first talking about what had happened. If not a scolding, if not a lecture, if not a heart-to-heart, we at least needed to share a chuckle over it. Over my surprise, and his too, probably, and over how I had dashed out of the house like an eleven-year-old. But I didn't want to talk about it with my father. I felt far too embarrassed for that. So we avoided talking about anything at all. We never painted the house together, either.

By the time the summer ended and I left for my sophomore year of college, I felt like an escaping convict. I was free from the prison, but still shackled to my troubles. I could never return there—at least not to enjoy the security and childish comfort I had felt for the first quarter of my life. The place just couldn't be my home anymore. Forever after I could be only a guest.

In that way the incident with Linda brought an abrupt and unsought end to my life as a full-fledged, integrated member of my parents' household. I guess you could say it was the way I acquired my independence. At least that's the way it happened the first time.

CHAPTER TWO

For a while afterwards diminishing little pangs of horror, embarrassment and regret dogged me. They returned most persistently whenever another sexual opportunity arose for me. That got to be a damn nuisance. The last impulse a man engaged privately with a woman wants to conjure is dread and embarrassment over his botched first encounter. But eventually the pangs grew weaker and weaker, less and less frequent, until one day, poof, they vanished. Unless I fished very deeply indeed into my memory, I could say that I had forgotten all about Linda.

But she roared back one day some fifteen years later, ambushing me on a morning I arrived late for my work. That event by itself was hardly remarkable. I had been coming in late all the time. In fact, I had been walking in late, I think, every morning since the students returned from Christmas vacation to start their second semester. That had been January, some five months earlier, and still every morning I found myself rushing to get behind my desk with only a few instants left to make myself look settled before my first appointment arrived. Chronic lateness is a sure symptom of advanced job dissatisfaction, a fact that I didn't freely share with my co-workers, though I couldn't hide the observation from myself. But what made this particular late-starting morning noteworthy was the fact that my secretary was late too. Usually she was in the office early, though I think just to chat on the phone. Well, I couldn't very well reprimand her for one late start. Not with my record. I breezed past her empty desk feeling annoyed just the same. I brushed through my office doorway but then I reared to a stop in mid-stride: A woman sat waiting in the chair facing my desk.

From where I stood I could see only her back, but she definitely was not Mrs. Tweed, my missing secretary. Silently I cursed her, Mrs. Tweed, for picking today of all days to come in late, when she should have been here to keep this lady out of my office, or at the very least to warn me that she was in here waiting for me.

"Hello," I announced from behind the woman, hoping the chill remained audible in my voice.

"Oh, hi," she said, turning to look at me over her shoulder and flashing a smile.

"Can I help you?"

"That's okay. You can go ahead and get yourself settled first. There's no need to rush on my account."

"I didn't know I had an appointment this morning," I said, plopping down in my chair, not looking quite at her, busying myself with some inconsequential paper mixing to make myself appear occupied. I'd get rid of her quickly for sure, I said to myself. But I'd have to stall for a minute or two until Mrs. Tweed arrived, so I could send the lady out to book an official appointment. Otherwise, if I sent her away before Tweed's arrival, I would have to hassle with the scheduling myself. I had never bothered to learn the secretary's scheduling system. I'm not altogether certain Tweed even had a system, or, if she did, if it was a system straightforward and logical enough for her to teach to someone anyway.

"Oh, I don't need to make an appointment," said the woman.

"Everybody has to make an appointment. I can't see you without an appointment."

"But I just need to talk to you a little about my son."

"Well, I figured that. But you still need to have an appointment."

"It won't take long."

"But if I saw every person who just walked in without calling first to make an appointment . . . " Mrs. Tweed had arrived. I heard her shuffling out at her desk. I was just about to call her in—to ask her to escort this woman out—when her hand snaked tentatively into my open doorway. It groped for the handle, then gently pulled the door closed. That was standard protocol. Confidentiality laws stated that the door was supposed to stay closed any time I was talking to anybody, unless I was talking to a teenage girl, in which case the door was supposed to stay open. But the door pretty much stayed opened or closed according to my or Tweed's convenience, the rules be damned. So why, I wondered with mounting annoyance, why did Tweed have to pick today of all days to become so damn diligent about the regulations?

"Look," I said to the woman, exasperated, "I can't see your son. In fact, I can't even talk to you about your son until I get a referral from his principal, or from his teacher at the very least.

That's the rule."

"You still don't recognize me, do you?"

I looked at her, really looked at her, for the first time since our circular conversation had begun: Linda.

Time and neglect had conspired against the lithe beauty she had possessed quite naturally as a girl. The pliant curves of her midriff were filled in now and the waterfall-turns marking her hip bones had disappeared. The taper had rounded out of her legs. Her fingers looked graceless now that a stolid meatiness had set into her hands. And her face, though not quite creased, wore a sullen grayness where past happiness, long distant, had washed out. Yet enough of the essentials remained: the high pointed cheeks, her slender, slightly pinched Gaelic nose, the forward thrust of her breasts (aided now, no doubt, by under-wires). There could be no doubt: this woman found waiting in my office was Linda. She had found me at last.

The sight of her again, so sudden and unexpected, obliterated all the intervening years of peaceful forgetfulness. My mind flooded instantly with all the fearful anxiety that had filled it during my nineteenth summer. I thought: this is it, that corner I just knew I'd turn someday to find her waiting for me, here to demand a reckoning face to face. I braced for the wave of mockery, abuse and reprisal about to break over me.

"I really thought you would," she said.

"Would what?"

"Would recognize me. I really thought you'd recognize me. But I guess it's no big deal. I mean, it's been a long time. I mean, a really long time."

"Really long," I reiterated.

"I would of made an appointment. But I figured you'd just recognize me and it'd be okay if I just came in to see you like this."

"Well, it's just that, if I had known you were coming, then I'm sure I would have recognized you."

"The thing is, I really have to do something about my kid. Right away. I really think you'll like him. His name is Trevor."

Trevor, I thought. If the kid was having problems it was no wonder, with a name like Trevor. Kids with nonconforming names could find it mighty tough to fit in with their adolescent peers, and to my mind fitting in with peers—or at least avoiding their jittery gaze—remained the best possible way to stay clear of the sort of school-yard cruelty that would create the problems that would land a student in here with me. And I was sure he was having problems, whatever the cause, because there could be no other reason why his mother would want to see me. I was the psychologist for the school district, which meant that the only parents I ever saw had kids who were ankle deep or maybe knee deep or even chest high in what at that moment were called adjustment disorders. Though they could have easily been called something else, given the regularity with which the profession reassigned names. Though the problems themselves never seemed to change that much. And the treatments or remedies or clinical approaches or whatever they were titled at any particular time remained as ineffective as ever. Renaming was a career I almost chose, toiling as a young graduate assistant at the university and seriously playing with the idea of staying there. Of becoming a learned researcher, which would have placed me among the leaders of the field, who desperately needed new subjects to cover for their new textbooks and for the recurring articles they penned for the professional journals, not to mention the occasional piece for The Atlantic Monthly, which are the very activities that helped delineate them as leaders after all.

But I had taken the opposite tack, abandoning my shady campus after my post-graduate studies and idealistically embarking on a career in clinical work. I thought I could do the most good in the world by greasing up every day to probe into real persons to try to set them aright. It turned out to be a big mistake. Approaching my subjects with a too-open mind, I found myself examining the results of my counseling on the level, eye-to-eye and maybe too honestly. Results can be very confounding, especially when an individual human psyche is concerned, because results are not often in synch with expectations. That was the weighty issue I now confronted after something less than ten years of practice. No matter how syrupy my intentions at the start, at least half the time I couldn't honestly say if I had made a person any better, or if I had actually made them worse. And in the cases where I could legitimately claim that a situation had improved, that is, when a patient got better, I couldn't honestly claim that I had contributed anything at all to the improvement. Maybe I did. But maybe the kid would have done just as well without me. I couldn't deny what I saw: there is so much resiliency already built into the human spirit, especially the juvenile spirit, which changes like the weather anyway. So was I really helping those spirits by sticking my beaming face into the works, looking for whatever little adjustment I might make? Maybe the kids would sort it all out automatically on their own anyway, sooner or later at least, without really needing my tinker's remedies. Worse, maybe I was only in their way. Maybe the built-in governors inside their noggins were simply too damn delicate, intricate and accurate for my clumsy hands to adjust. Maybe I was only throwing them all the more out of balance, no matter how good my intentions, so that my meddling actually impeded the cure. And that's the kind of thinking that led me to the most crippling doubt of all: maybe in the cases where I saw children get worse, maybe it was I, the civic-minded school psychologist, who made them get worse.

That was the sort of thinking that made getting into my office every morning for months so difficult. It had grown nigh impossible for me to face in good conscience the unscrubbed students the system kept flinging my way. I wanted to run from them—for their own good as well as for mine. Sitting through a counseling session I felt like a Tourette's sufferer with unmentionable utterances bubbling to get out of my mouth. I can't help you, kid. I don't have any answers. I'll only screw you up more. Your only hope is to tackle this thing on your own. Good luck, kid. I really mean that. But you're going to have to battle this beast solo.

That was my battered state of mind when I found myself facing the woman I had been trying to avoid through the prime years of my life. And here she was asking me to help her little Trevor.

Worse, I couldn't see how I could refuse to give her anything, everything she wanted. True, the cold panic I had felt just a moment ago had subsided. That was a great relief. But still I cringed in anticipation of the accusation she might aim at me at any instant, that I had slunk away in base cowardice, leaving her to fend for herself with my father in the house. How could I defend myself? Every inch of me felt guilty.

"The only thing is," I said, picking each word with care, "there's certain procedures I have to follow. Some of them are school regulations. Some are even state laws."

"What do you mean?"

"I mean I can't bring a student in for counseling just because a parent requests it. I mean, I can, but first you have to go through the proper channels. Everything has to go through the proper channels. In this case, that's the school. The first thing you have to do is schedule an appointment with your son's teacher. What's his name? Trevor? The first thing you should do is schedule an appointment with Trevor's teacher. Talk to her about his problems. Then, if she thinks it's appropriate, she'll ask the principal to write out a referral to see me. That's the only way I get to see individual students."

She sat simply looking at me with a lips-parted, eyes-blinking expression that I took, correctly, as a sign of confusion. That could only mean that I was winning. My confidence returned. I told her generously: "I'd like to just bring him in here on my own to talk to him for you. But our regulations are very explicit about that. What grade did you say he's in?"

"He's in eighth grade."

"Oh, junior high school. Then he doesn't have just one teacher you can talk to. What you want to do in that case is make an appointment with his homeroom teacher. Or, if you prefer, you can go directly to his principal. Either one is appropriate for a junior high student. We give you that flexibility. But, really, I need a referral from the school before I can even think about counseling him."

"But I don't want you to counsel him."

"You don't?"

"Of course not. What? Do you think my kid is some sort of a head case or something?"

"No. No. I don't think that. I didn't mean to imply that at all. It's just that, I'm the schools' psychologist, you know. So when a parent comes to see me I just naturally assume . . . "

"I just need you to let him stay with you for the weekend."

I didn't think I'd heard her correctly.

"You what?" I asked.

"I need you to let him stay with you this weekend."

"But I don't work here on the weekends. Nobody does. This place is totally deserted."

"I don't mean here," she said. "I mean at your house. I want you to watch him for me."

I had thought, after my few years with the school district, that I had seen every manner of sponging by members of what has grown to become the official sponging class, who are really just utilizing the helping professions, which, after all, are set up to allow for efficient sponging. But this was a new innovation.

"You mean you want me to baby-sit?"

"Not baby sit. He's fourteen years old. He can take care of himself. I just don't want to leave him all alone for a whole weekend. He makes too much trouble."

"What kind of trouble?"

"Just, trouble. You know. He's fourteen. Like, trouble."

"Oh, so, on my days off you want me to be a prison warden?"

"You don't have to put it like that."

"Listen, Linda" . . . I paused, checking the anger I felt spontaneously rising in my throat. After all, she still held her trump card. "I have to be very careful about my relationships with students. You see, there's all sorts of rules and regulations. They're there for their own safety and protection."

"I don't care about rules," she snapped.

"But I have to care about them."

"Why? I'm not asking you to do anything in any sort of, you know, official capacity."

"But, well, Trevor is still a student of one of our schools.

And as long as I am an official counselor of that school . . . "

"He's your son."

The words dashed into me with an impact so powerful that at first they didn't even register afore, in the up-front, thinking and acting layers of my brain. They passed right through, tangling up inside some down-deep, subconscious strata containing elements more substantial than my thoughts on the surface. Linda's words stuck fast against the diaphanous, little see-through man with his own arms and legs and head like a cartoonist might draw, the spirit part of me that's destined to wander the earth invisibly after I die, like Jacob Marley's ghost, except that instead of cash boxes my spirit will be shackled down with case files. He's your son. The words blasted against the little spirit man inside me and held him immobile, as if a powerful spirit wind had pushed him out of my body and stretched out all his limbs like four nibs of a kite, flailing and faltering helplessly, and the words held him there, frozen and suspended, pinned outside of my body, so that even his thoughts and warnings could not get through to the rest of me. That's how the Tourette's sufferer managed to keep control of my mouth for at least of few more ridiculous utterances.

"Even so," I said, "if I let him come stay with me I'd be opening myself up to all sorts of . . . "

"He's your son."

". . . all sorts of law suits and, and, other litigation."

"But he's your own son."

"What are you trying to say?"

"I'm saying that just because I've taken care of him for the past fourteen years doesn't mean that you don't ever have to do anything."

"My son?"

"That's what I said."

"He can't be."

"He is."

"I think I'd know it if I had a son."

"How could you? You ran off. Don't you remember?"

"You mean that day at my parents' house? That day we met in that little park?"

She looked at me archly, with an expression meant to convey that she knew that I knew exactly what she was talking about.

"But he can't. . . I mean, you can't. . . you couldn't have gotten pregnant then. Not by me. I didn't even, you know, we didn't even finish."

"It can still happen," she jabbed back. "And it did."

Silently I worked the numbers: my encounter with Linda happened, when? It was after my first year of college. I counted back to my graduation date, then added three more years. It happened fifteen years ago. How old did she say the boy is? Fourteen? But I would never name anybody Trevor.

"But I'm sure you would have contacted me, after all these years."

"What for?"

"Well, if I was really his father . . . "

"You were only the biological father. I didn't want you for the real father. And I sure didn't want you for my husband. I married somebody else."

"Somebody else?"

"Yeah. But he's not around anymore either."

"No. You can't expect me to believe all this."

She looked at me with a face that said that I knew that it just had to be true. If she was only acting, then she was turning in a very good performance.

"Listen," she said, "it's not like I'm asking for much. I'm not even asking for money or anything. All I want is one weekend. Then I'll never ask you for anything else ever again."

"But why all the sudden now," I demanded. "I mean, if he really was my son—and I'm not saying that he is—but if he really was my son, why would you come to me now after all these years?"

"Okay," Linda said, "I'll tell you the whole story. This guy I'm seeing right now, he wants me to go with him for the weekend to Atlantic City. He's paying for everything, so it isn't gonna cost me a dime. Do you believe that? Not a dime. That's just the kind of guy he is. I'll tell you, this is the best thing I've had going for a really long time. A really long time. Maybe it's the best thing ever for me. You don't expect me to take the kid along with me, do you? And I already told you I can't leave him home alone. And I can't leave him with my parents anymore because they're too old to watch the kid."

A small voice of indignation rose inside of me when I heard her call Trevor the kid. He was her own son, after all. She shouldn't call her own son the kid the way someone might flip off a passing comment about the car or the microwave or the mortgage payment. But why should I care what she called him? The question made my indignation rise even higher. I didn't have any interest in this, I said to myself, and I was going to be damn sure I didn't get paternalistic about a boy I'd never even seen before, no matter what wild claims were made about his origins. No matter who made them. The most I owed Linda was a simple apology. I certainly didn't owe her paternity. I didn't owe her a weekend of free baby-sitting. And what was I supposed to say to my wife about all this?

"C'mon," Linda pleaded. "It's not like I've ever even asked you for anything else before. And I'll never ask for anything ever again. I promise. It's not like I need to. I mean, I've gotten along fine on my own for all these years. It's just one weekend."

My job had given me glimpses at all the worst fiascoes people create for themselves, and therefore I recognized right away that this situation had all the ingredients needed to become the very worst variety. No matter what I said about it, no matter what conditions I placed on it, no matter what terms I demanded, my taking the boy might still be read as an admission of sorts, maybe even be used against me—and it could eventually come to this—in a court of law. Man, I thought with rising alarm, I've got to hie the hell out of this one.

"No," I said.

"But it's just for the weekend."

"I don't care how long it's for. I have a life too, you know. I have things that I need to use the weekend for. It's the only time I get to myself. You can't expect me to scrap all that just because you come in here on the spur of the moment and try to tell me that he's my . . . he's my . . . that I'm the father."

"He is your son."

"No."

"He won't be any trouble. He's old enough to take care of himself. He just needs a place to stay."

"No."

"I knew you'd be like this."

"I'm not like this," I said. "I'm not like anything. It's not me. It's the regulations. I'll be happy to see Trevor here, during the week, in an official capacity. Maybe I can help you out that way with any trouble you're having. But you'll have to get a referral from the school, like I told you before. I'll even help you with that. If you want I'll call Trevor's principal in advance. I'll call her right now, if you want. You can talk to her right away, on the telephone."

Linda slumped in the chair and folded her arms tightly across her chest. She crossed her legs at the thighs and started her suspended foot kicking, ticking really, as she stared with her head turned away from me out of the window.

"Try to understand my position," I said.

Still she looked away.

"I get parents in here all the time making all sorts of demands."

"I know where you live," she said.

"Yeah? So what? So you know where I live. What's that supposed to mean? What, are you going to send somebody there to break my legs? I've heard that one before too, you know."

"You have to take him," she said. "You can't expect to not ever have to do anything."

"Wait a minute. You're not saying that you're just going to leave him with me?"

"It's only fair."

"You can't do that."

Linda stood up.

"What about the boy? You can't just drop him off somewhere. He doesn't even know me. You don't even know me. You can't just leave him with a complete stranger."

She walked sharply to the door. I followed, shouting, "I could be an ax murderer for all you know."

She strode through the outer office and I kept after her. I said, "I won't take him. I won't be home. That's it. I'll go away. I can go to Atlantic City too, you know."

I glanced at Mrs. Tweed, whose desk sat off to the side. Then I looked back at Linda, who was heading into the hallway, getting nearer the exit to the building.

"Friday," she shot back at me. "Around supper time."

"I'm not going to stand for this," I said. I would have followed her down the hallway and even out into the parking lot but a new alarm began echoing loudly inside my head. It stopped me instantly. I thought: the hand that had reached inside my office for the door when Mrs. Tweed had arrived— there had been something different about that hand. But what was it? Now I remembered: its nails were painted a glowing red. But Tweed never wore red nail polish, unless . . . I glanced back at her. Yes, it was true, Mrs. Tweed had let down her hair.

Tweed had long, black, spiraling hair that ordinarily she wore twisted into a tight bun that she pinned to the top of her head. The only time she came out publicly with her hair brushed down over her shoulders and smoothed over her back like this was when she experienced what we on the guidance staff politely called an attack. During the last such attack she had been picked up by the police meandering back and forth across the busy Stark Road shopping strip, walking barefoot and singing Spanish melodies. Why she chose Spanish is anyone's guess. Mrs. Tweed is every inch a Protestant wasp, and not even an entire tub of self-tanning coconut butter could ever disguise that. Yet whenever her husband suffered particularly large gambling losses—at least I thought it was the gambling losses, because they correlated so closely with Mrs. Tweed's attacks, though, truthfully, no one was absolutely sure about what set her off —whenever her husband lost big in the gaming parlors, or even blew too much on state lottery tickets, Mrs. Tweed kicked off her shoes, peeled away her hose, combed her hair down straight and answered only to the name Carmelita.

Whenever she did, responsibility for coaching her back to sanity fell naturally to me. I shared the secretary with some other members of the guidance staff, but I was the only psychologist among them. That made me the only person the others considered qualified to handle what they so clearly saw as a psychological problem. I didn't mind the duty. In fact, it offered some special advantages. Tending to Mrs. Tweed meant I could cancel all my student appointments at least for a day, sometimes longer. And she was light duty. Typically her episodes as Carmelita ended with Tweed weeping somewhat over-dramatically in my office, a kind of grand finale which led me to suspect that maybe old Mrs. Tweed-cum-Carmelita knew exactly what she was doing all along. Maybe Carmelita was a put-on. Maybe her appearance was the distraction it took to snatch Tweed's husband back from the brink whenever the fellowship he enjoyed at the weekly Gamblers Anonymous meetings failed.

And all in all Carmelita was a pleasant woman, much easier to get along with than the ordinary Virginia Tweed. Ordinarily, Vina Tweed was a wide-eyed snoop ever eager to be scandalized. She was an Oprah fan, and I never could have come cleanly out of this loud duel with Linda under the nose of the real Mrs. Tweed. She'd grab her phone and start putting out the story, or, rather, an exaggerated version of the story, the instant I slunk back into my office. But now I gazed almost appreciatively at her—at Carmelita, I mean. By all appearances she didn't even know I was in the room. She hadn't even glanced over when I came charging out of my office, shouting after Linda as she had raced for the door steps ahead of me. Mrs. Tweed would have stood up to get a better view. But Carmelita sat unaware just several feet away, placidly humming the tune to Spanish Eyes (even in apparent madness it was impossible for Mrs. Tweed to escape her waspishness; to her thinking Spanish Eyes, the ancient pop single from the Italian Al Martino, was a real Spanish song). Her red-shod fingers were flying over the keyboard of a computer that, I could see from its blank screen, wasn't even switched on.

I stared back down the hall toward the exit: of course Linda was long gone. By now she had made it to her car and was probably even out of the lot. Well, I had a little time left to stew over her privately behind my desk. My office mates were still out on a morning round of meetings. I left Carmelita for them to discover when they returned. In the meantime I'd wait in my office, behind a closed door. That way, when they came in to tell me about her I could pretend it was news to me. I'd have to call in a temporary secretary right away, I realized, so she could cancel all my appointments and clear my calendar so I could attend to Tweed. With a little luck it would get me through until Friday.

I walked slowly back into my office and closed the door gently. I paused there for a moment, straining my ears till they picked up the chatty click of Carmelita's blazing nails on the keyboard. On my way past it I straightened the chair that had kicked back behind Linda when she had popped up so suddenly. I settled into my own chair. I closed my eyes. In the stillness I wondered again after so many years: so how did she make it out of the house?

CHAPTER THREE

Those quiet moments alone in my office supplied the soothing balm I needed. My shock, anger and surprise subsided
in the stillness. I calmed down a bit. After that I found it easy
enough to dismiss Linda's wild claim on my paternity. I'd been
the target of scams before. In fact, my job exposed me to all sorts
of fantastic claims from parents and students alike, especially
when circumstances weren't turning in a person's favor and
they needed a little leverage to bend them back. The modern,
savvy aid-recipient had experience enough to know exactly
what alarms would move him or her to the front of the line, and
certainly charging someone as a deadbeat dad, shirking on
child-support obligations, was a hot button of the moment, sure
to perk up anyone who heard it. But we aid dispensers had the
advantage of authority, which could make it tough to stick an
accusation against us. Heck, my job gave me an officially sanc-
tioned franchise over what got accepted as truth, a power akin

to what the medieval clerics once enjoyed. Therefore I dismissed Linda as just another parent pushing to open an escape hatch at the we're-always-here-to-help school system, which, after all, is in the business of offering escape hatches. She wanted to go to Atlantic City. She needed someplace to send her son. She found out one way or another that I worked for the schools and, presto, she had made me an instant papa. Why not? The dates matched up so closely that I couldn't absolutely disprove my paternity without doing a whole lot of troublesome checking, submitting to DNA analysis and the like, and who knew how long that would take.

Of course, I would have felt a lot more comfortable if the dates didn't match up quite so closely. In those quiet moments after Linda's visit I powered on my computer and pulled up the boy's records to find his birthday. Then I laid out the events on a calendar. Sure enough, granting a few weeks slack time either way to account for the uncertainties of conception and gestation, this boy's life could have begun on that summer afternoon when I was home from college and feeling bored. It had certainly started sometime that summer. Fortunately, all the other circumstances were too improbable. I was too much the social scientist to trust meddlesome coincidence, and the dates were just that: coincidence.

Besides, the sudden, unexpected visit from Linda had served as a kind of shock therapy, freeing me from her after so many years. She had simply gone too far. Maybe if she had stuck closer to my original fear, accosting me for running out on her and shaming me for cowardice, maybe then I would have succumbed to her. But instead she had hit me with such a fantastic claim that I could dismiss her out of hand as a crank. Now there was nothing left that she could throw at me. I was free.

But the weekend still worried me. On one hand, I thought that Linda's threat to drop off the boy was all bluff and bluster, a simple shout of anger because I didn't turn out to be the baby-sitter she wanted. No mother would really foist her child on a complete stranger, especially after the stranger had refused, so forcefully, to accept any responsibility for the boy whatsoever. On the other hand, she had to be pretty desperate to come to me with that fantastic story, claiming that the only sort of child support she wanted after, what, fourteen years, was a bed for the boy for one weekend. And in fact, I had seen a lot of mothers try to foist inconvenient children onto complete strangers. I decided it was best to conceive a plan, just in case she showed up on Friday with the boy. Of course I wouldn't accept him. If she brought him I wouldn't let him get out of her car, and if he got out anyway I'd put him in my car and follow Linda and make her take him back. As plans go that one was pretty simple, but it comforted me just the same.

I found it much harder to make up my mind about whether or not to mention the incident to Anne, my wife. Once upon a time it would have been easy, because once Anne and I had traded war stories pretty regularly. Not long ago the zany antics and surreal episodes we witnessed in the classroom and the counseling office were a regular part of our pillow talk as we chatted up late at night. The boy who stuffed peas up his nose during lunch to escape his afternoon gym class. Grubby little Bobby Feldrice, always too eager to play the big shot, who swigged urine from a small bottle when some of the sly older kids told him it was whiskey and dared him to drink it. The way Jeremy Butts, a poor kid, handed over the five dollars he'd found in the parking lot to Valerie Petrone for the pleasure of writing his name on her thigh. Anne was a teacher. She toiled in the junior high, which pitted her against kids in the most trying stages of their young development. The odor of over-ripened innocence is the scent that collects in a sixth-grade classroom after the lunch-time recess on the first hot day of spring. The children come in perspiring from all their secretious places that are just then opening into adulthood, a long journey ahead of them to be sure, with the lessons in adult hygiene among those that are still to come. The same discordant clashes between innocence and experience roil their psyches and emotions as well as their armpits. But there was a time when Anne took it all in better humor.

We had been married for two years, after meeting when I came into her homeroom to counsel the students en masse after a car wreck had wiped out one of their classmates. I had known the little girl who was killed, a quiet, almost cowering child who'd been sent to me for sessions when her parents were in the throes of a nasty divorce. She had come out of it okay, I thought, mostly because her good sense and intelligence—certainly the only real gifts that her parents, unwittingly, through the accident of genetics, had ever given her—were strong enough to triumph over damning circumstances. She was riding with an aunt, who was driving her, I think, to a piano lesson when another mom, late for a daycare pickup, skidded through a red light and T-boned their car.

Unexpectedly, surprisingly even, her death moved me. Before that I had been spared from any deeply sunk feelings of bereavement. The few acquaintances and some scarcely remembered relatives who had slipped away before this little girl had struck me more for their numerical significance, as mere population statistics. The most grief I could muster was pretty much perfunctory. Poor ol' Sydney's gone now; may he rest in peace.

But for reasons unknowable, this young person's passing tore into me as a personal and private loss. It left me for the first time with that hollowed-out feeling that comes once you comprehend that a piece of your life has gone missing forever. As predictable as it sounds, those over-worked words from Donne rang back into my head, and I understood, finally, their full-blown significance. Don't send to know for whom the bells toll. They toll for thee. I entered the grief-counseling session filled with passion. Of course, it was all but wasted on the kids in Anne's class. They were taking the tragedy the way kids that age always take one, with a lot of howling, a lot of eye rubbing, a lot of flat-out acting. They were just too young to legitimately comprehend death, though they had seen enough of life to know how they were supposed to act and how they were supposed to feel about it—I mean, they knew how we adults expected them to act and feel. So they put it on. I recognized right off that the clique of girls crying the loudest for their fallen classmate, the ones in the of-the-moment, gem-colored shoes and the small-bodiced blouses, the group of girls most precociously developed in viscous sexuality, were also the girls who had teased their classmate most maliciously, most incessantly when she had still moved among them. Probably. Cynicism comes along as an uninvited companion to insight. I had seen too many of these situations before.

Still, I carried my passion into the classroom that day. I turned the hour into a stirring eulogy for the dead young girl. Naturally it produced the opposite result that grief counseling is supposed to produce. Instead of settling down these kids—most of whom, as I've noted, were already pretty cool about the whole affair anyway, no matter all their howling and gnashing—my session stirred them to a deeper appreciation of the loss than their tender ages entitled them to. Some of them cried sincerely after that. Apparently I stirred Anne too. We began dating. Within a year we walked together to the altar.

Back then we would have laughed at a school story about a woman trying to trick me into baby-sitting. In bed at night the laughter from such stories tremored through our bodies and relaxed us, the prelude to kisses, which we could always count on as preludes to sex.

But a while ago Anne had stopped listening. In fact, she'd told me flat out to stop bringing my troubles home from work. She hadn't seen them as troubles before. But maybe I hadn't presented them that way before. Maybe by now my stories had turned into bitter excursions in bitchery and Anne was simply tired of hearing them. Or maybe she was trying valiantly to reform me, by getting me to cut back on the complaining. Maybe she just wasn't up for the laughter. Maybe she simply didn't want to have sex anymore. Maybe she just didn't want to have it with me.

So what could I say to her about Linda's threat to drop off her son for the weekend? If I warned Anne about it and then it turned out to be a false alarm, and I was certain—almost certain—that it would turn out that way, she'd claim that I was just overreacting to a parent again, that I was simply collecting more reasons to dislike my job. She'd tell me that I couldn't really expect some woman to send her son here for the weekend. (Make no mistake: the part about Trevor staying for the weekend was the only part of the story I debated telling my wife; I never even considered mentioning Linda's account of how he came into the world.) On the other hand, if I said nothing to her, but then the boy arrived and Anne watched me star in a spectacle with Linda in our driveway . . . well, I couldn't imagine how

Anne might react, or what Linda might say to her if she found the chance. As unlikely as that possibility seemed to me, I decided to err on the side of safety. I decided to mention it to Anne, treating it in an offhand manner, like one of our old anecdotes that I was telling her more for her amusement: you won't believe what happened to me today.

I waited until Friday afternoon, when we were both home from work. I suppose I should have told her much sooner, but I just couldn't stir up enough energy—or perhaps enough bold-ness and cunning—to make the words come out of my mouth until it was so late that I couldn't possibly wait longer.

"You wouldn't believe the mother I had to fend off the other day," I offered.

"I wouldn't?" said Anne, really only half listening from the couch, where she had plopped down to read the newspaper, her usual home-from-work relaxation ritual.

"She insisted that I baby-sit her son for the weekend so she could go away."

Anne looked up, regarding me.

"Is this someone you know," she asked.

"No. That's what I mean. This was the first time she'd been in to see me."

"Really? But you've been seeing her child, right?"

"No. Never."

"Wow," said Anne. "That is a strange one." She turned her attention back down to the newspaper spread out on the cush-ion beside her.

"Actually," I continued, "I did recognize her."

Anne looked up at me.

"We went to high school together. But I never really knew her. In fact, when she came to my office it was a while before I even knew who it was."

"She must think she knows you pretty well," said Anne, "to want to trust you with her child for a whole weekend."

"I don't think trust mattered a whole lot to her. She just wanted a place to dump him."

"But of course you said no."

"Of course," I assured her. "Although, she did say she was going to drop him off anyway. But that was while she was storming out of my office. I don't think she really meant it."

"Are you sure?"

"Yeah. She was real worked up at the time. I think she was just venting."

"Who is this lady?"

"I don't know. I told you, I don't know her. Her first name is Linda but that's all I can remember. I don't think I even knew what her last name was back in high school."

"Well what grade is the kid in?"

The kid. Once again I rankled—unexpectedly—at the term.

"Her son is in eighth grade."

"Eighth grade!" exclaimed Anne. "Why didn't you say so?"

I hadn't said so because I hadn't intended the conversation to go this far. Anne taught science at the junior high, and therefore odds were good that she would know him, or at least know of him. When I was planning this out I had decided that it would be better if the discussion didn't get into anything like this that might prolong it.

"His name? I think she said his name was Trevor."

Anne's body seemed to lift momentarily off of the couch.

"You don't mean Trevor Winkle, do you?"

"Well, as a matter of fact, I think that is his name. Yeah. That's it. It's Trevor Winkle."

"Trevor Winkle," she said. "Her son's name is Trevor Winkle! If you ever let Trevor Winkle into this house . . . "

"Take it easy," I told her. "There's no way I'm going to let her leave the boy with us. It would be incredibly unprofessional for me to let any parent do that. I told her that. I told her we wouldn't accept him under any circumstances. I'd be opening myself up to a lawsuit or something."

"Trevor Winkle," exhaled Anne, exasperation ringing in her voice.

"So you know him?" I asked the obvious.

"I wish I didn't. He transferred into my B-section just a couple of months ago. Yeah. I think that's right. I think it was just two months ago. It must be one of those broken-home situations where he relocated from someplace far away. At first I thought it would be tough on him—coming to a new school so late in the year like that."

I recognized the peril in the fact that this involved Anne's precious B-section. In fact, if I had known there was a connection, I never would have started the conversation. Since the beginning of the school year last September my wife had cared about nothing except her experimental B-section. It had been billed as another bold new approach to education. In this one, certain slow students and certain fast students were selected to share the same class. According to some feats of reasoning that I was never able to quite comprehend, the mixture was supposed to allow the students to learn faster than they would if their class was made up of only bright kids or, conversely, of only the dim ones. The key was supposed to be in the group dynamic that was sure to ensue, and the formula for making it work was to select just the right slow kids to mix with just the right bright kids. Call it disposition screening. The concept added up to an irresistible, no-lose situation that any education bureaucrat would love. First, it assured work for the bureaucrats, since a lot of administrative effort went into picking the right mixture of kids. Secondly, it made every parent happy. Even parents of over-achievers would be pleased that their heirs were progressing faster than the kids in the ordinary honor classes, which is exactly how the program was sold to them. All that was needed to make the theory a full-blown educational practice were a few field trials to absolutely prove that it worked. Anne's B-section was one.

"So, what's he like," I asked her, confounded by a curiosity about the boy that was stronger, apparently, than my defensive impulse to shut up, to let the subject drop and move on to a discussion less volatile. Still, I cringed secretly at the noise of the question parting my lips.

"He's diabolical. He corrupted the whole class."

"He can't be that bad," I said. "You make him sound like he's Satan's spawn."

"I think that he is. He's at least a little Satan in training. It took me all year to finally get the right balance in that class. To get all the up-level kids working well with the down-level kids, and vice versa, just like they're supposed to. Then they stuck him in because he tested out with the up-level group, believe it or not. I haven't been able to get anywhere since."

"Why not?"

"Because he's eroded my authority. That's why not. He's one of these too-cool kids who challenges everything, but then he comes off like he doesn't care about anything when I try to correct him. There's no way that I can get the best him. Now he has the respect of the class—or at least of the down-level kids in the class—instead of me. He's divided them. And now they're all starting to behave like that, too. Everyone in that class is just too cool now to be bothered. It's terrible. He's terrible."

Or it might have been that Anne was trying to blame the failure of this bold new concept on a late-coming kid who provided her with a ready excuse. But a trouble-maker or two has always been a part of the teacher's burden. How could she expect any class to be free of at least one, even a class that had been screened for dispositions? Dispositions turn out different-ly in different situations anyway, which makes something like a group dynamic rather tough to engineer, no matter what the high-flying theory stated. I had recited that argument to Anne before the school year had begun, when she had first been offered the class. She didn't buy it then. Why would she listen to me now? And why would I want to repeat it now anyway? Why would I want to keep alive this conversation in order to defend Trevor Winkle from being scape-goated, as I suspected he was, at the risk of inviting Anne's fury upon myself?

As it happened, her fury visited me anyway. Before I had even a scant moment to consider my options in this little talk, Anne snapped her attention toward the window like a wary Doberman that scents an intruder. She gazed outside with shock, surprise, alarm. Then she stood up abruptly, anger ignit-ing her eyes. She banged across the floor toward the kitchen, banged open the swinging door and disappeared behind it. I rushed to the window to see what it was: a kid was walking up the driveway.

I had never seen him before. Still, there was no mistaking who it was. Trevor looked unremarkable, like every other boy of fourteen that particular season: baggy jeans, black sneakers, longish hair cut straight all around to just below his ears, so that it domed his head like a mixing bowl turned bottom-up. I rushed out the front door to intercept him.

"Where is she," I demanded.

Trevor stood in the driveway silently, following his first instinct, which was to clam up.

"Where is she," I repeated.

"Where's who," he answered at last.

"Linda. Your mother. Where is she? I didn't even see a car."

"Who are you," he asked, and I just glared at the insolence.

"Are you Dan," he asked me.

"Never mind who I am," I said. "It doesn't matter. Come on. You're going back with your mother." I strode quickly down toward the end of the driveway, as though I expected the car to be there, as if I just needed to get a little closer to see it. Of course nothing materialized. I looked back at the boy, still standing in the driveway near the house where I'd left him. "Where'd she go," I snapped at him.

"Are you Dan," he asked back.

"Yes. I'm Dan. Who else would I be. Now where's Linda?"

"She's not here She never was. She dropped me off a little ways down the road."

"Which way? That way?" I demanded, pointing.

"Yeah, I think it was that way."

"Come on," I said. "You're going back with her." I walked back up the driveway, quickly, striding past him into the garage to my car. Trevor stayed in the same spot. I waved my arm insistently for him to come. He did, finally, being careful to appear unrushed, the far pole from how I must have appeared to him.

Of course, no sooner was my car down the driveway and the wheels spinning away from the house than I realized how ridiculous the chase was. She was long gone. I had no idea where she lived, and even if I knew, she probably wasn't going home anyway. She was probably driving straight to Atlantic City, or to a rendezvous with the boyfriend taking her there. I drove on anyway, now just to save a little face, or at least not look quite so damn foolish to the boy sitting beside me, his flimsy backpack stacked on his lap, his eyes turned out the front windshield, as if he was only out for an afternoon sight-see. Or maybe, like me, he was watching in the vain hope that his mother's car would magically materialize in front of us and he could escape in the damn thing.

"It looks like there's no way I can catch up with her now," I said at last, speaking because something simply had to be said to puncture the silence hanging between us. I never expected to feel so uncomfortable with him. After all, I had sat with hundreds of kids one-to-one just like this. Maybe it was because we were in my car, my own car, rather than in my office, where the setting and circumstance were crafted for me to control.

"I figured she would have at least come to the door," I said. "Introduced you or something. Given me a chance to tell her that I just can't take you for the whole weekend."

Trevor shrugged. "I don't know. I think you should just take me home," he said. "I can tell you how to get to my apartment. You can just, like, leave me there."

"Will your mother still be there," I asked hopefully.

"No. She was heading out right away. But I'll be okay by myself. It's not like it's a big deal or anything."

"For the whole weekend?"

"Sure. I stay by myself all the time."

"But not for a whole weekend?"

"I used to. The only reason she won't leave me alone this time is because some of the neighbors turned her in. She had to see the social worker. They were going to charge her with, like, abandonment or something."

I drove on further, not knowing what else to do, feeling like I couldn't turn back, feeling that I didn't have any place to turn back to, or anywhere else to go as long as this boy was with me. We were stuck out here together, citizens of the highway.

"She told me you'd be expecting me," he said. "She told me you were an old friend of hers and she'd set the whole thing up in advance." Those words, I think, were meant to stand as an apology, or as close to one as a kid in his position can come. I was surprised by my own, well, tenderness, when I realized with unexpected alarm how uncomfortable he had to be feeling, no matter how hard he tried to conceal it. I would have said something, so that he wouldn't have to carry the full burden of the conversation alone, and so he could see, maybe, that I wasn't in a full fury anymore, but I could think of absolutely nothing to say.

"It's okay if you, like, just take me home," he repeated. "Really. I'll sneak in so nobody will see me, and I promise I'll stay out of sight for the whole weekend so nobody will even know I'm there."

I bumped the car down onto the shoulder of the road to get enough turning clearance to swing it around in a one-eighty, and I pushed back toward home. How mad could Anne be, I reasoned. By now she'd already had a little while to cool down. By the time we made it back to the house, she'd certainly be ready to agree that this just wasn't my fault. It wasn't Trevor's fault, either. Linda was the villain here and Linda was long gone. She'd duped us both, both the boy and me. She'd told us stories meant to trick us into accepting this arrangement that neither wanted. What could anyone do about it now? I couldn't exactly leave a fourteen year old to fend for himself. Anne would understand that. So what if she held a grudge against this particular fourteen year old. I felt sure she wouldn't expect me to turn him out onto the street.

Once inside the garage I told the boy to wait in the car while I went to smooth things over with Anne. I found her in the kitchen, going over some student papers on the table, her red pen clenched so tightly that her knuckles blanched white. She fixed her eyes on me.

"Did you get rid of him," she demanded.

"Well, not exactly."

"Then where is he?"

"He wanted me to take him home but he would have had to stay there alone. His mother is already gone."

"So, what are you saying? Are you saying that you brought him back here to stay with us?"

"No, not necessarily."

"Then where is he?"

"I just need a little bit more time to figure out where I can take him."

"He's in the car still, isn't he?" Not waiting for an answer she burst up from her chair and banged out the swinging door. I stood in the kitchen still, watching the door oscillate in and out, in and out, in and out of the room on its spring. Then from over by the other door, the door leading to the garage, I heard Trevor say, "I'm going to hitchhike home."

"I told you to stay in the car," I snapped at him. Too late: Anne was back through the swinging door. She held a small travel bag, stuffed rotundly. Apparently she had packed it in advance, while I was out with the boy chasing Linda.

The two faced each other squarely now from opposite sides

of the room, me smack in the middle. The boy gaped. "Mrs. Hectorman," he exclaimed. Then he recovered a bit. He looked blankly away from her, as though there was something else he should be paying more attention to. Anne never so much as glanced at him. She aimed her full-bore, double-barreled glare at me and said, "either he goes or I go." Then, as if to prove her sincerity, she strode brusquely in front of me, pushed past Trevor, and disappeared into the garage. She brushed by him so closely that he had to hop aside to let her pass. But even then she did not look at him. From the kitchen I watched through the window as her car rolled down the driveway, then spun away out of sight.

"That's my science teacher," Trevor said at last.

"That's my wife," I added.

"I'm not staying here," he said.

I loaded him back into the car and set off for my parents' house. He wasn't too keen on the idea of staying there, either. He asked me again to take him home. He said he'd hide out. He said I could even let him out right on any street corner and he'd hitch home on his own. I drove on, and despite all his protests he assured me at last that he'd stay put at my parents' house, complaining bitterly about the neighbors in his building who had turned in his mother when they caught him alone. If it happened again social services might claim custody of him. He was afraid they'd shuttle him off to a foster home. "I'm not ever going to let those people take care of me again," he said before he lapsed into a brooding silence.

That left me to brood privately on the thought that taking him to stay with my parents was also a very stupid idea.

CHAPTER FOUR

My mother suffered from Alzheimer's disease. The erasure of her memory had begun a few years earlier, just as my parents crossed the threshold to that misnamed period, their golden years. It was subtle in the beginning. At first she began to show signs only of simple forgetfulness. She left her purse in the washroom at a restaurant. After boiling water for tea she forgot to turn off the burner, leaving it cranked to an ominous orange. She didn't set the timer when she started a cake in the oven. Then she forgot about the cake entirely, until its burnt, black edges smoldered enough to trip the smoke alarm in the hallway. Domestic stuff. Easy to dismiss at first. But the weight of evidence grew steadily heavier. In conversations she repeated questions, sometimes asking the same one three times or more in the span of a five-minute chat. She messed up names, starting at first to forget only casual acquaintances but then seeming stumped often even by the face of an old friend. Playing parlor games she couldn't keep track of her turn. She needed to ask, always, about the rules.

On the day that I arrived with Trevor, her Alzheimer's had by then advanced to the state where it left her little more than idleness and emptiness. At times she seemed simply vacant. Other times she talked and even acted as though she was experiencing events long past, from her childhood even, because those were the only images she could find in her memory. At least she seemed contented then. At other times her eyes sparked from the fear of displacement, looking out at an unknowable world from which she felt separate and detached, dispossessed even in the place where she most belonged. The failure of her mind, the slow erasure of her memory cut her free from any comfortable familiarity with places, objects, people. Her own home, her own kitchen, her own bed, at times even the man beside her in that bed, all looked new and unfamiliar to her each time she viewed them, because she could not remember them from the last time. Except during the glimmers of recollection that visited her now very infrequently, she felt totally alone in the world.

But at least she abided it quietly, living as a small, wizened woman drawn back into solitary, fretful observation. Not so my father. He stirred around endlessly in a fit of unrelenting agitation. Peter was coping very poorly as a care-giver.

That was a surprise, because Peter had always seemed to be such a capable person. Adaptable, too. As a young man he had made a go of it as a portrait painter. For a short time he even lived the whole bohemian, starving-artist routine, before finally going to work as an illustrator for the daily newspaper, a job he stayed with until retirement. He kept at the painting as well, but it became a hobby, something he fit in after his daily toils for the union-negotiated paycheck. His marriage to Elizabeth, my mother, came a little late—for people of their generation, at least. Along with the newspaper job, it cemented him into a predictable domesticity that survived even the appearance and upbringing of a child, me. Peter's problem now, I think, came from the fact that Elizabeth had provided all the order and symmetry that he had come to take for granted. Her sense of duty, her acceptance of sacrifice, her sheer love of hands-to-it labor established the daily rhythms, the household routines and rituals that had lulled Peter through comfortably to retirement. Supper always waiting. The paper always in from the box. Then it all collapsed with the collapsing structure of Elizabeth's mind.

When we arrived I told Trevor to wait in the car. Everything was fine, I assured him. This would be a good place to stay, I told him. It would just be easier, I said, for me to explain everything to my parents first, before I introduced him. Trevor took this speech impassively, looking away as if there was something more interesting going on outside the car window, almost straining to convey that he didn't care one way or another. But as I climbed out of the car I noticed his eyes turn and follow me.

I found my father inside the house, pacing feverishly back and forth across the living room rug, while my mother, eyes wide forward like a frightened deer, watched him from a chair.

"It's a good thing you're here," he said as he saw me come in. "He's at it again. This time it's worse than ever. He must really be off the deep end now."

He could only mean Glen Watts, the neighborhood bully who, as luck would have it, lived right next door.

"Why," I asked. "What happened?"

"It's Elizabeth I'm worried about. You know what she's like these days. There's no telling what . . . she was always afraid of him before. Now who knows what . . . "

"Settle down," I said. "Tell me what happened."

"It's him. He went off the deep end again."

"When?"

"Just now. Just before you got here."

"Why?"

"Why? Who knows why? Because he's crazy. That's why. There's never any reason with him."

It was true: there never was a reason, or any other reasonable way to understand and explain Glen Watts. He was no garden variety bully. In addition to his inborn meanness, he also seemed to suffer spasms of psychotic activity that appeared unpredictably, though all too frequently. At these times his envy of the greener grass across the street, his anxiety over painting his house (Watts had begun painting his place a woodsy green some seven years earlier, really, and the job was still unfinished), his running quarrels with every person around him, his seething hatred of dogs and bicyclists and passing cars, all his uncountable dissatisfactions bubbled into frothing outbursts that sent Glenn Watts running into the street or charging into a neighbor's yard to try to provoke a brawl. "This is going to come to blows," he'd vow. Or, "I'm going to punch you in the mouth." But for all that, I never actually saw Glenn Watts in a brawl. He threatened a lot, to be sure. But it was the same as his yet-unpainted house: his intentions never quite translated into any discernible results. After issuing his threats and loudly invoking body parts by their locker-room names, after thrusting out his chest, shaking his fists, squeaking more unspeakable vulgarities and kicking up all sorts of dust, after every outward show of belligerence and hatred, his fury would simply subside like a sigh. After that Watts would skulk back to his yard, and spend the balance of his day scowling over at you and muttering more unspeakable obscenities. The pattern made it easy to dismiss Glen Watts. Dismissing him was the best defense. His neighbors had learned that if they engaged his rages, it simply prolonged the tantrum. Instead everyone ignored him.

"He came running right out at me," father said. "I was just mowing the grass. Minding my business. Then he came running out there to the edge of his yard."

"Why didn't you just ignore him?"

"He threatened me. He said this was going to come to blows. That's just what he said: come to blows. He said he wasn't going to take any more of it."

"He always says that."

"This time he meant it. It was different. I could tell. He said he wasn't going to take any more of it."

"Any more of what?"

"My lawn mowing. He said he didn't like the way I was mowing the grass. He said I blew the grass clippings onto his property."

"Oh, dad," I chided. It all sounded like vintage Glen Watts to me. He yelled at neighbors all the time about cutting their grass, usually when the growl of the mower woke him from a nap.

"It's not me I'm worried about," father said. "It's Elizabeth. I don't care what he says to me. You know that. But you know how your mother was always so afraid of him. Who knows what she must think of him now."

Actually, Elizabeth had been first in the neighborhood to identify Watts as a harmless crank. Through the years she had enjoyed a lot of laughs at his expense. But I knew it wouldn't do any good to correct my father. He wouldn't hear it. Silently, forlorn and in need of distraction, I looked out through the window, gazing in the direction of the diminutive Watts estate. The lawnmower stood where my father had left it, between the two houses, out near the border of the lot, at the spot where, I guessed, he had fled the assault. Watts was outside still, fiddling under the hood of his pickup truck. He wore the green janitor pants that were his signature, presumably because to him they signified serious work. Watts never seemed to change clothing. He was a big, ungraceful man with a small, round head. He'd had been married twice, but both women had left him, neither daring to give him children before her escape. Now he lived alone.

"You know better than to pay any attention to him," I said to my father.

"I couldn't help it this time. He was ready to attack me. Literally attack me. He would, too. You don't know what he's like anymore. Lately he's gotten a lot worse than he used to be. All the sudden. I don't know why, but he has."

"He looks about the same to me," I said.

We didn't notice Elizabeth rise and go to another window. She cut into our conversation: "What's Danny doing out there?" We both turned and looked at her.

"Ma, I'm right here," I said.

"It's okay, Elizabeth," said my father in exaggerated consolation, like a shout at a person with a hearing aide. He went over to her, put an arm around her shoulder and turned her back toward her chair. "See what I mean," he shot back at me. "I don't know what she's thinking anymore. All she does now is look out the window. Then she repeats the same question over and over and over again. That's all I ever hear. The question of the day. Over and over. Then she acts like she's a little girl back home again. She doesn't even know where she is. You don't know what it's like around here anymore. It's crazy."

"We've talked about this before," I said, hoping to calm him. "It's the disease. You know that. You know she can't help it. You know it doesn't do any good to get upset about it."

"Now this happens. Damn that fat bastard Watts. He really got to her this time. Now I don't know what to do with her."

"If anything got to her I think it was you," I said. "I don't think Watts had anything to do with it."

"Who the hell is that?"

"What? Where?"

"Out there. That kid walking around in the yard."

Trevor. He was strolling, kind of meandering in the side yard that bordered Watts' lot. He walked under a tree and looked up into its canopy. He went over to the clothes pole, the ancient, steel, tee-shaped pipes supporting now only a single, limply low-hanging and unused line running back from the house. He rubbed a finger over the pole's rust scale. He wiped the finger on his pants.

Instinctively both father and I looked over at Watts. He had stepped away from his pickup and stood exactly as we expected, reared up with hands on his hips, lips parted a bit but otherwise his face squished down into a squint that showed disdain, disgust, even, yes, hatred for this boy who had zoomed into his sights, a boy he had never even seen before.

"Who is it," asked father.

"That's who I came to see you about."

"You know that kid?"

From the clothes pole Trevor headed over to the doghouse, a dilapidated, rotting wooden box stuck back in the far corner of the yard. My parents hadn't owned a dog in years, and the sad doghouse showed its age. Watts stepped out menacingly from the front of his garage, coming around to the side so that he could keep Trevor in full view.

"I don't really know him," I said. "I met him today for the first time."

"Then what did you bring him over here for? You know better than to bring anyone over here. Not the way things are now. Especially with what's going on here today. Now where's he going? That kid's gonna get himself killed."

Trevor walked along the border of the yard, just a few perilous feet off of Watts' property, heading toward the mower my father had left abandoned on the lawn. Watts, meanwhile, had ducked into his garage. He re-emerged carrying a rake, then cut a straight path to the edge of his lot, positioned to intercept the boy just before he reached the mower. Watts started raking with conspicuous fury, another pattern of his, raising small puffs of dust where he scratched into the ground. The rake was simply a decoy, an excuse for him to stand menacingly in a spot where the boy couldn't possibly miss him. He glared hard at Trevor, jerking the rake up and down but not moving it from the spot where it began to dig in like a tiller.

But the boy brushed past him coolly, not so much as glancing at Watts. Trevor bent down over the mower, unscrewed the cap to check the gas, replaced it with a few casual, deliberate twists, then ripped back the pull-cord to start the machine.

"I had to bring him here," I said. "It's a bit of a long story. He goes to the junior high. Anne has him in one of her classes. Plus I'm supposed to start seeing him for counseling. That's why he can't stay with us. It would be too much of a, you know, a conflict of interests."

"What do you mean, 'stay with you'? Stay with you for how

long? You don't mean that you're going to leave him here with us, do you?"

"There's no where else I can take him."

"For how long?"

"It's just for the weekend."

"The weekend! Are you crazy! You can't bring someone here for the whole weekend. Think how upsetting that would be for your mother. We don't even know this kid."

Trevor mowed to the end of the row my father had left unfinished. He turned around and began working his way back up toward Watts. This was the dangerous pass, because the mower's side chute pointed toward Watts' yard, tossing the spent grass just inches from the lot line. Maybe a few clipped blades would even land on Watts' shoes where he stood savagely scratching the earth. Watts stopped raking entirely. He leaned forward and glared hard, hard, hard at the approaching boy. As Trevor pulled abreast of him, Watts let loose with soul-piercing shouts. We couldn't quite make it out over the drum of the mower. Still, it was easy enough to imagine the string of curses, obscenities, threats and insults he hurled at the fourteen year old. Yet Trevor pushed the mower calmly past, without so much as a glance toward his attacker.

"That kid looks awfully familiar," my father said. "Who did you say his is?"

"He doesn't look familiar to me," I answered. "I told you, I don't really know who he is. It's a job-related thing: there were some family problems and I got stuck with him for the week-end."

"What kind of problems?"

"I can't say. You know: client confidentiality."

"He's not in any trouble, is he?"

"No. He just needs to stay someplace for the weekend. That's all it'll be. Just one weekend."

"But not here," father said. "You don't know how bad it gets around here anymore. I don't know how much more I can take. I really don't. Elizabeth doesn't do anything anymore. She doesn't cook. She doesn't clean. She can't even carry on a conversation anymore. Everything I say goes in one ear and out the other. Hell, I don't even know if it's going in anymore. If I tell her something she forgets it before I'm even done talking to her. And then she asks the same questions again and again and again. She always thinks she lost her purse. She doesn't even have a purse. Remember? You said I should hide it."

"But dad, she's been like this for a long time already."

"Then she loses things. Important things. Every day I have to keep her distracted when I think the mailman's coming. I can't even let her see him come. Then I have to rush out there before she does. If she gets the mail she puts things away. Loses them. Bills. Everything. And I can never find them."

"We've been through all this before."

"But I don't know how much more of it I can take."

Trevor was returning with another pass of the mower. Watts worked himself into a spitting frenzy. He slammed the rake onto the ground. He stamped around in a little circle, a kind of involuntary spasm, then he stepped to the very edge of his lot. The property line was easy enough to distinguish. My parents' side was green and grassy still, especially now, in May, even though it had been neglected somewhat these past two years of Elizabeth's illness. But Watts' side had known decades of neglect. The plants grew in small, withered clumps and patches on hard-packed soil. Watts inched forward as Trevor approached, compelled to more spasms by his rage. One foot stepped across to the grassy, green side, so that he straddled the property line, one foot on his, one on ours. His hands were closed tightly into fists thrust down straight at his side. His whole body leaned forward, impelled. His chin jutted outward, though his face otherwise closed into its pig-eyed squint.

"I told him he should stay in the car," I said as we watched Trevor come calmly apace. He pushed to mower up even with Watts, stopped, turned it off. Watts was like a stretched elastic string at the point of its violent snap. But Trevor walked calmly out from behind the mower, crouched over the machine and pulled the pigtail wire off the spark plug, a move right out of the safety manual. He stood up again, walked just as calmly around to the other side of the mower—so that now he was actually facing Watts—crouched and reached into the shoot to clear out a sodden clog of grass clippings.

With the machine switched off we could hear Watts clearly now. "You little fuck," he hissed at the boy. "You fucking little prick asshole. I'm going to kick your fucking ass. Stand up, you little fuck-sucking asshole. I'm going to kick the fucking shit out of you right now."

The odd thing was, the mower didn't appear to be clogged at all. The clumps Trevor pulled out looked too small and insignificant. But he stayed coolly at the task, reaching under the deck with the measured, deliberate care of a surgeon. He didn't even glance at Watts, who seethed just a few feet away.

"Get up, you fucking little dick-weed fucker. Get the fuck out of here or I'm coming over there right now to kick the fucking shit out of you."

Trevor stood up.

"And you better not come back, ever, you fucking little shit."

The boy stepped behind the mower's handle, yanked back the starter cord—oops: he bent to reconnect the spark plug, yanked the cord again to start the motor and pushed on calmly toward the end of the row.

Watts strained to go after him. He looked stuck, feet epoxied to the ground but about to break loose. He pulled up, pulled up, strained his body forward, spasmed as if a great chill or a shock of electricity or an orgasm had passed through him. Then he turned abruptly around. Watts stormed away, closing his hands again into little fists and stomping his feet as he pounded back to his garage, walking for all the world like Yosemite Sam, the cartoon cowboy. He left the rake where he had thrown it, out by the edge of his yard. He disappeared inside his house for the rest of the day.

"Why in the hell is this kid cutting my grass anyway," my father mused.

"Danny does such a nice job with the lawn," said Elizabeth, who had risen to the window again.

"Mom, I'm over here," I said.

"At the speed he's going, it'll take him another two hours at least before he finishes. What did you say his name is?"

"It's Trevor. Trevor Winkle. He's not a bad kid. Kind of quiet, that's all. He's only been in our school a couple of months, but there's no record of him getting into any serious trouble."

"But the way your mother is right now—I got my hands full already."

"It looks to me like maybe he can help you get caught up on some things."

"You just don't know what it's like around here anymore. She's gotten a lot worse lately. I'm just—augh." His speech trailed away into a groan of desperation. I didn't have a response. We stood silently at the window a moment, shoulder to shoulder while Elizabeth looked out another. As we watched the boy work, the scent of fresh-shorn grass wafted into the house, filling up the place with the young, bounteous, juicy green odor. It was a synesthetic stimulant: I recollected how much I used to enjoy cutting the grass here. I mowed as slowly as Trevor now went back and forth across the yard. The chore was a sop for anxious teenage energy, because it preoccupied my muscles, setting them to work with a sense of clear purpose. Yet its easy rhythm and repetition weren't really strenuous enough to distract me. That left my mind free to wander across the splendid fantasies of adolescence: saving lives at the beach, scoring touchdowns, dressing to turn my friends' heads, the bodies of women. Then, at the end of each row, as I turned around and started back, I liked the look of my work's progress, the flat, even columns etched into the fragrant lawn, and I felt satisfied by the labor.

I agreed to pick him up Sunday afternoon at dinner time to drive him home. That would get him there before the time he said his mother was due back from Atlantic City. I wanted her to find him at the apartment, so that she wouldn't come poking around my house to fetch him. When the time came on Sunday Trevor directed me to the building where they lived. It sat out on a suburban shopping strip, a little two-story apartment building with a ridiculous mansard roof, the whole affair set conspicuously close to the road—conspicuous at least among the grocery stores and shopping plazas that had grown up around it, all of them standing far back behind parking lots the size of lakes. The owner of this tired little box of apartments, as anonymous as always, had given up patching, plastering and painting the building a few years ago at least. It looked as if he was waiting now to be bought out by a filling station or a Dunkin Donuts or some other, more appropriate business establishment that would level the place and start anew. As we drove into the building's cramped lot I stepped the car slowly over potholes and crumbling asphalt. I nosed it into the only open space, between a rust-perforated, old Ford LTD, a dinosaur car, and a little Toyota faded to the color of cornmeal. The cars mirrored the attitude of the building, lonesome and weary, like the sagging doghouse pushed far back into the corner of my parents' yard. I wondered, what now, or, more specifically, how was I supposed to say goodbye to the boy. I understood implicitly that I would never see him again, and the thought made me unaccountably melancholy. Layered on top of that came a flash of hot annoyance over the melancholy. What did I have to feel sorry for? After leaving him Friday with my parents, I hadn't even seen Trevor again until now. And, face it, it had been I who had done him the favor, not the other way around. Still, I felt compelled to pack him off at least with the standard male salutation, the firm handshake, meant to convey masculine affection as much as it disguises deeper feelings. The question that had me stumped was, should I do anything more than that? Certainly not a hug. But maybe I could give him a, hope to see you around some time, or why don't you look me up this summer. The problem with those was the worry that he might really look me up. His appearance this weekend had caused trouble enough. I wasn't keen about asking for an encore performance.

Lost in this complex of emotions, I was slow to realize that the woman I'd watched walk out of the building and cut over toward us, the woman now crossing in front of my car and peering in through the windshield with a surprised and startled grin was Linda. With one hand she lugged a couple of green plastic garbage bags laden low with clothing or bedding or the like. In the other she held some dresses and shirts on wire hangers, flung awkwardly over her shoulder. Clearly she hadn't been expecting us. She'd been caught in mid flight, and now she scurried faster, walking bent kneed in her hurry to put down the load before the weight pulled her down. She went round the old LTD parked beside me and tossed the stuff over the driver's seat, into the back, the clothes on hangers scattering across the car.

So where the hell is she going now, I wondered. Trevor popped out of my car, saying only "see ya later." He might have said the same to a bus driver. He hustled around to Linda's LTD. She dropped it into reverse before he even had his door closed. He's not wearing a seat belt, I thought to myself. She zipped the car back, swung it around behind mine, churned the tires a turn as they felt for a grip against the crumbs of asphalt, then surged off toward the back of the lot. The LTD moved like a fat lady, a hard lean around a slow right turn, low dips to the side each time a tire stepped into a hole. Except for the spots where the rust pocked through, the car was a dull, flat, uniform gray. Primer gray, meant to be covered by paint, sprayed on years before by someone who forgot to finish the job as casually as you might forget to turn off the light in the basement.

My impulse said follow her: catch up with her car and demand an explanation. An explanation of what? Of why she left Trevor for the weekend? Of where she was escaping to now? Of where she'd been and what she'd done with the boy these last fifteen years?

In the back corner of the lot Linda bumped her car down into two dirt ruts crossing the weedy strip of earth that separated hers from the large parking lot, freshly paved, of a new

Wal-Mart. I watched the LTD lumber away, picking its way amid the few parked pickup trucks and minivans, some scattered shopping carts, the heaps of soda cups and crumpled McDonald's bags shooed from cars. I half expected to see a tumbleweed roll by. This was Sunday, round about closing time. The spirit of the weekend was vanquished. The place had a ghost town look. I could have lived forever without ever making good my obligation to Linda—whatever that obligation might have been. But now, ready or not, I had repaid the lingering debt. I was free from her at last. I watched her big, rusting auto roll toward the back of the Wal-Mart lot, probably making for another unpaved, unauthorized escape road. Awkwardly, leaning like a fat lady unsure of her balance, the car disappeared around a rear corner of the building. I started my own car, and pushed on toward home.

CHAPTER FIVE

I managed to feel some smug satisfaction for the tidy way I had tied up the whole ungainly incident—though, I had to admit, I owed as much to dumb luck as to any shrewd maneuvering on my part. Still, Linda hadn't succeeded in saddling me with the boy an entire weekend. I had pawned him off. But at the same time, he had helped me diffuse the crisis at my parents' house. In fact, things there had turned out much better with the boy than they would have turned out if I had gone there alone—and it's certain that I would have ended up there that weekend in any event. Given the panic my father was feeling when I had walked in with Trevor on Friday, there can be no doubt that he would have called me. But as it turned out, bellicose old Watts hadn't reappeared again the rest of the weekend. Probably he felt too embarrassed after losing his showdown with the boy. Whatever the reason, his disappearance alone was enough to salvage the situation. But on top of that, my father's grass was mowed. His car gleamed from a washing and a waxing. Some of the clutter in his garage had been rearranged so that at least it looked more orderly. And, finally, the decaying dog house had been dismantled, the debris cleared away. Who would have thought Trevor would turn out to be so industrious? Who would have expected a fourteen-year-old kid to possess such skills? I couldn't even remember the last time my own car had been washed, let alone waxed.

My wife, Anne, remained the one sore spot that prevented me from gloating too completely. I never expected her to congratulate or even to thank me for getting her problem student out of our house. But I certainly thought she'd be around at least to see what I had accomplished. Anne stayed away the whole weekend. She didn't return until Sunday night, coming in around bed time, hours after I'd deposited Trevor at Linda's apartment. Her little bag hadn't seemed full enough to support her for three whole days.

She breezed in Sunday night as if nothing had happened. By that time I had already resigned myself to another restless night in a bed that seemed too damn big, a night of dozing and waking and wondering, when suddenly I startled to the sound of a push at the kitchen door downstairs. I heard her keys go jingle and clunk as she tossed them onto the table, Anne's customary, welcome-home habit. I listened to the drop of footsteps unmistakably in her cadence. I braced for a tussle as she entered the bedroom, but Anne breezed through to the bathroom without saying a word to me, without even glancing at me, without a smile, without at least a scowl. She went through her nightly wash-up as casually as if she had just come up from watching television in the den one floor below me. Back in the bedroom she started for her pajamas on the hook behind the door, but she caught herself halfway there, and pulled them instead from her little travel bag. As she climbed into bed she said only, "Is the alarm set?" I rolled my back to her and closed my eyes to try to sleep.

We talked the next morning before leaving for work, but it was all bland information, bereft of anger and strife. I learned that when she had left me Friday Anne had gone straight to Susan's, where she had more or less planned on staying Saturday night anyway. Susan, a friend, had planned a bridal shower on Saturday for Gwyn, Anne's sister, who was getting married the following weekend, a storybook May bride. Anne and Susan and Gwyn, along with some members of what Anne called her old gang, had figured they'd turn the shower into a junior-high-style slumber romp. It was true: Anne had mentioned the sleep-over earlier in the week, but I had forgotten all about it. At the time it had sounded too tentative, the sort of activity planning that required more confirmation before a husband would bother locking it into memory. I guess I should have listened to her more carefully, I said. Anne explained that she had tried to call me Friday to say that she was spending the night, as well as Saturday night, with Susan, but I didn't answer the phone. But I wasn't home to answer the phone, of course, because I got tied up at my parents. She would have left me a message, but of course the answering machine didn't pick up, because, apparently, I had dashed from the house in such a rush with Trevor that I'd forgotten to turn it on. But I scarcely ever turned on the answering machine. I didn't like the damn thing. Anne knew that. She should have tried harder to contact me. I told her that. "After all," I complained, "we'd just had a big fight."

"I wouldn't call it a big fight."

"But you walked out of here. You packed your bag and

everything."

"The bag already was packed, practically. I was already planning to go to Susan's the next day. I just went a day early."

"But you could have told me. You had to know I'd be worried and upset after the way you left and everything."

"I tried to call you. I already told you that. I called you and you weren't home."

"You could have tried again."

"You could have called me at Susan's."

"But I didn't know you were there."

"Then you should have listened to me when I told you about our plans for the shower and the sleep-over and everything."

"But your plans were for Saturday. You left Friday."

"You could have figured it out if you stopped to think about it for a minute."

I made it to work early that Monday, the first time in memory that I beat my office mates to the place. As I arrived I felt a tug of eager anticipation for the few soothing moments of quiet solitude that awaited me before the workday began. I'd start the first pot, I figured, and suck in the heady smell of the coffee as its narcotic scent infused the entire guidance suite. But I walked in to find the lights already ablaze, the coffee already drip-brewing, and Carmelita hard at her computer. At least this time she had turned on the thing. She looked to be going over the appointment schedule, probably mopping up the mess that the rest of us had made in Mrs. Tweed's absence the week before.

I was surprised to find her here. It was early, after all, well before starting time, and Tweed never made it early into the office. She usually beat me by just a few minutes, but that was when I arrived barely in time for my first session, which could be thirty minutes into the day. But this wasn't Tweed. It was Carmelita, and I hadn't expected Carmelita to reappear at all. I had expected the attack to have run its course by now. That was the usual pattern. After only a few days of Spanish Eyes and self-tanning cocoa butter, Tweed always returned to resume her duties with her usual feint at diligence, acting as if the mysterious Latin woman had never displaced her. Yet here sat Carmelita still. And she was working. In the past she may have found her way into the office, but she never managed a stitch of work. The new Carmelita who beat me in the door Monday actually seemed to be functioning as the guidance staff secretary. She stayed in that role, arriving every morning as Carmelita the secretary as we moved through the week.

Of course, she couldn't match even the low level of office efficiency that Mrs. Tweed maintained. Carmelita's nails—long red press-ons that humped unnaturally from the tips of her fingers—made typing much slower. And she wandered, sometimes, around our little office suite, drifting into the halls and through the other administration offices nearby. Curiously, she never went into the high school itself, which was attached. The new Carmelita even stole brazen siestas, dozing at unpredictable times in her office chair, her head thrown back, her mouth wide open, her arms crossed and resting on her protruding gut. Her loud snoring unnerved the guidance counselors tremendously. Especially Alice, a thin slip barely out of school herself and therefore still too naive and trusting to maneuver around so many of our wily high school students. One morning mid-week Alice hustled out of her office to greet a student coming in for a skull session and led the lad into her room by the hand, trying to block the slumbering Carmelita from his view with her body.

It worked, until drowsy Carm sucked in an enormous snore, then clapped her jaw to resettle her restless tongue.

It would have been easiest to simply wake her, but Carmelita's apparent madness made Alice and the rest of the counselors too timid to take any sensible actions. Instead they followed my cues, and I was happy to let her sleep. I didn't have to watch her as closely then.

The new Carmelita remained on the job until Thursday. I arrived early again that morning to find the lights extinguished, the coffee pot cold, Tweed's computer blank. By then it had gone on long enough anyway, and I decided it was time for me to take some more affirmative action to get Tweed back. I made my first-of-the-day batch of java at last, then waited in restful solitude for the others to arrive. When we had all assembled I announced that I was heading out to find Carmelita. That meant setting a new and, probably, unwelcome precedent: a psychologist making a house call. But at least I got to cancel all my student appointments for the day.

Vivian and Alfred Tweed lived in a smallish house in an early post-World War II neighborhood in which all the houses were smallish, built to the same floor plan and evenly spaced on smallish lots lining arrow-straight streets, so that the houses lined up as neat and orderly as soldiers at drill, or as bowling pins to people unaccustomed to marching. Each house was an ersatz Cape, a pointy-roofed cube standing a story and a half, cozy, with a nook of a kitchen off the side door, the kitchen opening into a dining nook, that opening into a living room, leading back to the two downstairs bedrooms, but not before you passed the closet-sized bath across from the stairs that went up to the half-story top floor. The Tweed house and all its look-alikes had gone up in the burst of speed and economy meant to satisfy the domestic yearnings of returning soldiers, and also the yearnings of the women who had awaited their return so eagerly. Private, affordable homes with their own driveways, they were the payoff to the night-and-day individualists who had united to undertake the Great Adventure. But through the fifty-odd years since the war, the scatter-shot of individual desires had rubbed out most of the uniformity in the Tweeds' neighborhood. The buildings retained their rank and file spacing and their Monopoly-house outline. But now some had protruding front vestibules attached. Others stood before big add-on garages. Some cowered within wary fences. Still others hid behind fleets of cars: three, six, eight even, spilling out of the driveway and onto the curbside and some, even, parked in the front yards. There were houses with aluminum siding gone chalky. Houses covered with garish vinyl slats. Houses with faux-brick fronts. Some with pink feather-stone pasted low along their cinder-block foundations. Some had tiny, checkerboard lawns. Still others sat on hard-packed dirt. All in all the place had gone shabby, wearing the cluttered, jumbled, anything-goes garb of tough-luck culture.

Yet the Tweed house stood out for its neatness. In fact, it was fastidiously neat. The siding—vinyl siding like all the better houses on the street—gleamed with a whiteness that could only come from regular washings. The same applied to the aluminum awning over the front stoop, supported by black iron poles rising from black iron railings ornamented with twists and curly-cues and little metal leafs, the whole affair coated in glossy Rustoleum. This was my first time here, and as I bumped the car into the driveway—recently sealed with paint-on tar—I noticed how the lawn lined up against the asphalt in straight-edged obedience, shaping out a perfect little rectangle that Pythagoras might admire, bounded on one side by the driveway and on the opposite side by the walk leading up to the Tweeds' front stoop. Across the walk another perfect rectangle of grass ran up to the edge of the neighbor's driveway. It was the edges I admired, trimmed razor straight. They told me that the lord of this house had to be a serious compulsive. But I had never noticed anything approaching a compulsive streak in Mrs. Tweed.

She met me at the front door before I even rang the bell. Seeing her indistinctly in the shadow behind the screen door, I couldn't make out which woman greeted me, Carmelita or Mrs. Tweed. She seemed to be stuck somewhere between the two. She wore the red press-ons still, but her hair was pinned up into Tweed's customary bun, the first I'd seen of it in more than a week.

"Did you call me a little while ago?" she asked me through the screen.

"We tried."

"I heard the phone. I figured it had to be you."

"Well, it was all of us."

"I guess I should've answered it. It's just . . . I . . . well . . . I figured I'd see you in the office soon enough anyway. I meant to come in. I've been trying to get dressed all morning. I guess you might as well come in now that you're here."

Done up as Latin Carm at the hands but waspish Tweed at the hair, and wrapped elsewhere in a generous housecoat, she led me to the cramped dining nook off the kitchen, where she dropped heavily into a dinette chair. I settled slowly across the table from her. The inside of the house was done up with as much fussing as the outside. The shellacking still gleamed on the honey colored kitchen cabinets that were dotted with big black pine knots, a style I remembered from my childhood.

High above the sink, on a valance made from the same wood, their names were neatly etched: Viv 'n Al. Was it a confirmation, or a hope?

"I guess I should offer you some coffee," she said.

"That's all right."

"Do you want some?"

"Only if it's not too much trouble."

I'd already noticed the full carafe steaming on the squat Mr. Coffee machine. It looked just made, but Tweed didn't get up from the table.

"It's not really necessary for you to come to work today," I said after a moment. "I mean, if you're up to it, then it's okay. But don't feel like you have to. I didn't come over here to get you or anything like that. We were just a little concerned about you. Because we know you haven't been feeling well lately." By now I could see that I was talking to Tweed, not Carmelita, forget the red nails.

"You thought I might've taken a whole bottle of sleeping pills or something, right?"

"No, nobody thought you'd do anything like that. We just thought you might want someone to talk to."

"If I wanted to talk to someone I would have answered the phone."

"Yeah. I guess you're right. That's the problem with telephones. You can't not answer it and still expect the person at the other end to know what's going on."

"I didn't know it would turn out like this," she said. "I mean, I wanted to come to work this morning. I even started to get ready." She splayed her fingers to examine her nails, the red press-ons lapping over the tips like fish scales. "I can't talk about this," she said, closing up her hand and drawing it in and tucking it beneath the other against her gut. "It's too embarrassing."

"Well, I'm certainly not going to pressure you into talking about something that you don't want to talk about. You know that. But it might make you feel better. If you're ready for it, I mean. Besides, how can it be more embarrassing than going around dressed like Carmelita? You've told me before how foolish that makes you feel, when it's all over, I mean."

"But at least I can't help that. It's a sickness, isn't it?"

"Can you help the other thing?"

"What other thing?"

"The thing that's bothering you. The thing you don't want to talk about."

"No. I guess I can't. I used to think I could. But now I guess it's pretty clear that I can't."

"At the office we always thought that it had to do with your husband's gambling."

"You know about that?"

"Not really. I mean, nobody knows any details or anything. It's always been just a suspicion. I don't know how it got started."

She pushed herself up from the table and crossed with effort into the kitchen. In turn she tipped each of the three cups on the sink's drainboard, looking inside each, before she took one and rinsed it under the faucet. She drew a heavy breath. She poured in coffee, then took a heavy breath. She pulled a plastic milk jug from the refrigerator (breath) and poured a dollop into the coffee (breath). She slewed in an avalanche of sugar. While it was poised inverted above her cup I read the word SUGAR printed neatly in big block letters with a black marker on the side of the plastic dispenser. What else could it have been, I wondered.

"You probably know all about compulsive gambling already," she said, settling back into her seat with a heavy breath, taking a shaky slurp from the coffee, anticipating its heat.

"I've read about it," I answered. "And I certainly know about compulsive disorders, as we call 'em. But gambling is one that's a little bit outside of my specialty."

Actually, that wasn't entirely true. By this time articles chronicling teen compulsive gambling were starting to crowd some of the kid-shrink journals, so I could have been up on the disorder if I had bothered to read any of them. But I'd seen so many next-big-things wash through the profession that by now I'd been desensitized. Who could feel differently? All such latest findings, no matter how loudly heralded, were always based on surveys anyway, and if working in my field taught you anything, you learned that the least reliable way to find out about the habits of bragging, swaggering, image-conscious adolescent child is to ask them. Besides, Tweed was talking about her husband, somewhat of a codger, which, according to the laws of specialization, disqualified me on all accounts.

"He's been at it for years," she said. "Not constantly. There's been times when he stops and goes on his best behavior. Sometimes it goes on like that for so long that you almost forget all about it. You forget he ever had the problem in the first place. We get all caught up on the debts and everything. Sometimes we even get some money saved up. Then something always happens." Tweed stretched out her fingers and regarded the flaming nails of Carmelita.

"Did I ever tell you that once we were all ready to move," she said. "We'd finally saved up enough money. We had a new house all picked out and everything." She lifted her head and gazed around us, at the fifty-year-old honey-colored cabinets in the kitchen, at the square-walled living room too small for the furniture crammed into it, too small for the big, long couch, for the Barcalounger, the big TV in a big cabinet pushed up against a wall. She looked at the heavy curtains closed tight against the encroachment of neighboring houses too near at hand. "I shouldn't still be living here," she said.

"It looks like a very nice house," I said. "It's certainly well taken care of."

"Alfred does all that."

Of course, I thought to myself, it's Al who's the compulsive.

"He even does the cleaning now. Why shouldn't he? He's retired. He's got all the time in the world. Besides, he's the one who spent all our money. I could be living in a nice place by now. In a nice neighborhood."

"Where is your husband," I asked her.

"I don't know where he is. That's the problem. I shouldda seen this coming. He started coming and going a little while ago. I knew something was up then but I didn't say anything. I shouldda stopped it then. But he just disappeared one day last week. I already knew he was gambling again, because he'd been laying awake the whole night just thinking about it. You can't be married to a man for nearly forty years and not know what he's thinking about when he's laying awake in bed at night pretending to be asleep. It was the same old thing all over again, him lying in bed the whole night thinking so hard I swear I could hear what he's thinking. Like, where was he going to get the money from. How was he going to cover his tracks. How was he going to make the big bet, win that big bonanza he's always talking about. It's always been the big one with him. When he gets going he wants one big win. Then he'll quit. That's what he says, anyways. Problem is, no matter how much he wins it's never big enough. He figures the next big bet will pay off even more. So he just keeps on going, and then of course he ends up losing everything."

She pulled another long slurp from the coffee.

"This time I don't know where he got the money from. He doesn't have any of his own. Hasn't for a long time, either. Everything's in my name now. The house. All the credit cards. The checking account and savings account. Everything. Even his retirement check comes by that direct deposit now. He can't even get the money out. Only I can. So don't ask me where he came up with it. All I know is that he came up with some money somehow. And when he gets back here there's going to be hell to pay. You mark my words."

"Then are you sure he's gambling? I mean, with all the precautions you've taken and everything . . ."

"It's not like I chained him down or anything."

"Well, yeah. But still, to be gone a whole week—has he contacted you at all."

"I haven't talken to him since the day he disappeared."

"Maybe something happened to him. Maybe you should file a missing person report."

"You mean with the police?"

"Of course."

"Why?"

"Because maybe something happened to him."

"Hah. That would only give him the satisfaction of thinking that I care about him. I already know nothing happened to him. I'm sure of it. I know he's off betting someplace, and the only reason he hasn't come back yet is because he knows what he's going to get from me when he does."

"What if he doesn't?"

"Oh, he'll come back all right."

"Maybe, with all you just said and everything, maybe he's too afraid to come back."

"What, you mean like maybe I should try being nice to him? I've already been plenty nice to him. Besides, how can I do that when I don't even know where he is? How can I do anything? Besides, he doesn't deserve me being nice to him. Not after what he's put me through. And I don't just mean this time, either. Listen," huffed Tweed, "there's no way in the world you can know what it's like until you've been through the mill. I mean really through the mill. We had twenty thousand dollars saved up. It was more than that, really. It was more like twenty-two. Twenty-two and some change. But twenty was all we needed to put down on the house we had all picked out. We were going to use the rest to buy furniture and stuff. Nice furniture. Then we were going to sell this damn place and put that money away for our retirement nest-egg. Our retirement! Hah. Now here I am, working still. How many people do you now who are working still at my age? They get to retire early. Not me. He blew it all. I remember that day like it was yesterday. After all sorts of haggling the people selling the house we wanted finally accepted our offer. We were all ready to go to the bank to get our mortgage and everything. It was a bargain, too. You can't believe how happy I was. But when I go to get the bankbook it's nowhere to be found. I look in there and there and there and there. And he's looking right along with me. As though it's only misplaced. As if he doesn't know where it is either and it'll turn up if we just keep looking. He'd lost the money weeks ago."

"He lost twenty-two thousand dollars?"

"Every rotten cent of it."

"But how?"

"The usual way. For all I know he could of blown it all at the state lotto shop. He can go through hundreds of scratch tickets alone. Sometimes he even wins a pot. But then he gets all worked up and starts betting on sports. Once he loses some he's got to bet again so he can get his big win that's going to cover all his losses and even have some left over so he can come out looking like a hero. Alfred Tweed, the big wheeler and dealer. And look at him, living here with me."

"You think he lost twenty-two thousand dollars like that?"

"I know he did. Because it wasn't the first time or the only time, either. And you can bet it was more than twenty thousand, too. It might have been fifty thousand, or sixty thousand, because he can win a lot when he works at it. But he always ends up losing it all over again because he can't ever stop. If only he'd take some of that money home before it was too late. I'd of made sure he didn't gamble it all away again."

She was like the lady alcoholic who resented her man's drinking when it made him an angry, belligerent drunk, but appreciated it when he was a charming, cuddlesome drunk.

"Don't you have any idea where he might be," I asked her.

"None whatsoever. He's never left me like this before. Not for this long. But you know what? I don't care. Carmelita might have cared, but I don't give two hoots. Not two hoots. When he comes strutting back in here I'm going to throw him out on his ass. Gambling is one thing. But walking out on me like this is a whole different ball game. And if I find out that he's been shacking up with another woman . . ."

She turned over her splayed hand so that the palm faced upward. She scrunched it tightly into a fist. But it was a girl's fist: instead of crossing her thumb down low against her fingers, she capped it along the open curl at the top. When I was a kid you got ribbed if you made a fist like that. You'd break your own thumb, the tiny roughs would say, if you ever hit anyone with a fist made that way. Of course, the theory went untested. Boys talk a lot about fights. But one rarely, sometimes never happens.

"The one thing I'll never stand for is him being with another woman," Tweed went on. "He can treat me like dirt. He can keep me here in this pigsty. He can piss all the money away I make for him. But if I ever catch him with somebody else . . . "

"I'd hardly call this a pigsty."

"I'll kill him," she said. "I'll kill him and I'll kill her. I'll kill 'em both. There's not a court in the world that would convict me. Not after what I've been through for him."

"You could always plead insanity," I said.

"They can give me the chair, for all I care. But him with a honey: no way. That's the one thing I'm not going to put up with."

"But you don't really think he's gone off with another woman, do you?" I'd met Al Tweed, and I couldn't imagine it.

"No," she answered, but it was clear that she did believe it. There's much self flattery in the thought that others want the mate that you've got.

"I'm sure he's just off gambling some place. I'm sure it's nothing worse than that. Maybe he's in Atlantic City. Well, maybe not Atlantic City. But maybe he's gone to Foxwoods or someplace like that. He can't stay forever. He has to come back. Soon. How long did you say he was gone?"

"I don't know. About a week."

"Well then he's got to come home soon."

"What makes you so sure of that?"

"Well, just look at this place. There's everything a man

could want right here."

"He's never been gone this long before."

"He'd be a fool not to come back."

"He's been a fool plenty of times before. Plenty."

"I think you just need to give it a little more time. There's no sense jumping to conclusions until you know exactly what's going on."

"You really think so?"

"Of course."

"And you really think he'll come back?"

"I'd put money on it."

For the first time almost since we'd started our chat, Tweed shifted her focus away from her nails. She looked down into the front overlap of her housecoat, a billowy affair of flimsy cotton that had begun, from fatigue no doubt, to sag open. She seemed to realize with a shudder that it was all she was wearing. She wrapped the neck more snugly and cinched the belt tightly enough to make her exhale audibly.

"I was just getting dressed when you came," she said by way of apology. "I thought you were the mailman."

"I wish I was," I smiled to lift her, "if you greet your mailman at the door every day."

"I'm not usually home," she said, patting her high-stacked hair to check the construction of the bun. "He should be coming soon. I really didn't mean to keep you this long."

"I don't mind. I canceled all my appointments. We can talk some more if you want."

"No. I mean, I feel much better now. I really do. I'll be into work in just a little while. I was going to come in anyway. Later. I was just getting dressed and it was taking me longer than usual."

"Are you sure? I mean, you can take the rest of the day off if you like. It's not like I came here just to fetch you back to the office." Although my best hope had been that she would come back willingly—come back as Tweed, that is, not as Carmelita. After about a week of Carmelita's sub-standard performance, the place needed straightening out. So I didn't object again when Tweed insisted she return today. I didn't have time to object anyway. She all but shooed me out the door, assuring me she'd be on my tail, racing into the office just as soon as she got dressed. But as I left I passed the mailman coming up the front walk. He was whistling and stepping jauntily, though he stopped and appeared startled when he saw me come out of Tweed's door. He eyed me challengingly as we passed. Tweed never did show up at work that day.

CHAPTER SIX

Another reason Anne came back so coolly Sunday night after our fight the Friday before, or rather, after what I had taken for a fight, was the wedding. In fact, as the week smoldered on, I realized that only the wedding could explain her willingness, after the long climb up the stairs to our bedroom and through every subsequent moment since then, only the wedding could explain Anne's willingness to signal surrender—or to signal at least a truce—in the battle that I had feared was just getting started. Anne would want me on my best behavior at the wedding. She'd want the two of us to absolutely ooze an aura of marital happiness, because with her family, family bliss counted as an asset, and the healthy rivalry between Anne and her sisters and her brother ran strongly enough to make her want to display many assets. She realized, I'm sure, that we'd never pull it off if we strung last weekend's tiff through this week approaching the wedding of her sister Gwyn.

So we remained tersely cordial through the week, all the way to Friday, the day of the wedding rehearsal and the vaunted rehearsal dinner. Anne took the day off to prepare, but I worked a full shift. I had good reason to. For one thing, I wanted to make sure Tweed returned in good order after playing hooky the day prior, and I wanted to see for myself that it was really Tweed who returned, and that Carmelita was neatly folded and stashed in a bureau drawer. It was owing to Carmelita, after all, that I had fallen so perilously behind in my current project, which gave me my second ready excuse to work the Friday of the rehearsal. Through the weight of an official memo from the Office of the Superintendent (an office just an eraser's hurl down the hall from the guidance suite I occupied), I had been instructed to draw up the guidelines for courtship and hand-holding in the district's elementary schools. That followed the Supreme Court's split decision in a case called Davis v. Monroe County Board of Education, which cleared the way for little kids—well, for the parents of little kids—to sue schools if a little kid claimed to be sexually harassed by, well, another little kid. The best way to avoid such a suit was to stamp out pre-pubescent flirtation altogether, and the task of drawing up the new guidelines for teachers to follow fell to me, the school psychologist. Presumably that would make the guidelines more sensitive to students' feelings, though it was hard to imagine what could be sensitive about stamping out flirtation.

Nonetheless, I needed a solid day at the office to start, and to finish my recommendations. Gwyn's rehearsal festivities weren't starting until the evening anyway. And the only part that really concerned me was the dinner, which would begin later yet. Anne was matron of honor, but I was only attached.

Gwyn's intended husband came from a family of well-todos, the long-established variety of American aristocrats who shelter money from the government tax taker and who use the savings to support their tenured memberships at golf and tennis clubs. For the customary, post-rehearsal dinner the groom-to-be brought us to the chandelier-lit private-party room of a well appointed, dutifully attended, good-cooking restaurant. Yes, the food was memorable. But my dearest recollection of the evening came from Gwyn, bride-to-soon-be, who delighted me during the meal by the artful turn she performed in her chair as she stretched toward me across Anne's lap, who sat between us, almost reclining atop her sister's thighs, to extend her empty wine glass to me so that I could replenish it from my glass, which seemed to be always just refilled. Befitting her status as the feted maiden, Gwyn wore a dangerously low-cut dress that fell open the further from her sidelong bend. From the radiant smile she flashed up at me while I sloshed a pour half into her glass, half onto my own flattered thigh that supported Gwyn's hand that supported her glass, I could see undeniably that the effect of her attire was calculated. I swam in the compliment.

And who can doubt that it was Gwyn's exhibition, plus the wine that elicited it, which awakened my appetite for Anne that evening? Sometimes it takes an external flame to melt off the layers of inhibition and indifference that accumulate between a man and woman no longer recently married. I felt the bedding impulse prowling between Anne and me in the quiet of the car as we drove home. I prickled in the woman's presence as we entered our still and darkened house together. In the bedroom I waited with quiet intensity. But Anne came out from her nightly wash-up throwing signals that looked all wrong.

"I think the dinner went pretty well," she said with too much day-is-done finality as she climbed into bed beside me.

"I certainly had a good time," I said.

"That's a great restaurant. We'll have to go back there."

I rolled onto my back and locked my hands behind my head: a clear message that I wasn't ready for sleep.

"Just how much money does Brandon's family have," I queried.

"I don't know. But it has a lot more than mine."

"I guess Gwyn is making out a lot better than you did."

"Don't be silly," she said.

I wasn't being silly. I was simply trying to keep the conversation alive, and feeling a twinge of desperation to do so as I noticed in the furthest reach of my consciousness the very start of the onset of alcohol's second most welcome effect, which was its threat to pull me down effortlessly into sleep, which is its consolation prize.

"I guess tomorrow is going to be a busy day," I murmured.

"I don't even want to think about it."

"Don't worry. I don't think anything can go wrong now. You and Gwyn have planned it all out too carefully."

Anne rolled onto her back like me, so that each of our voices now shot upward in parallel paths toward the ceiling, and mingled there, but left us separate down below. You don't have to worry about bad breath after booze, because the alcohol cleanses or maybe just masks.

"That's the part that worries me most," she said. "You know how it seems like the more you plan, and the harder you want everything to go perfectly, the more certain it is that something will go wrong. I just hope it's not something big."

I rolled onto my side, facing her. I threw my arm across her chest, an exploratory gesture. Anne slept without nightclothes.

"What could go wrong," I asked her.

"Anything can go wrong."

"Well, what could go wrong that you would consider something big?"

"Oh, I don't know. Something like Brandon leaving her standing at the altar."

"It's more likely that Gwyn would leave Brandon," I said. "She's had more experience at it."

"That's not very nice," Anne protested, pushing away my arm that crossed her.

"I was only kidding," I said, although it was true: Gwyn had abandoned her first fiancé at the altar. But that had been a youthful affair, an infatuation with a bewiskered singer and song writer. He ended up clean shaved and working in the financial sector. I spotted him manning a booth at a mall sometime after the aborted wedding. He was hawking stocks or mutual funds or some kind of financial service to passers-by.

"I just want her to be happy after everything she's been through," Anne said. Gwyn was Anne's younger by about eight years, and my wife's concern for her ran decidedly toward a big sister's, or even a maternal concern.

"Don't you think she's happy already?"

"I don't know. I hope so. But it's so hard to tell. It's so hard for anyone to be happy."

"What do you mean by that?"

"You know what I mean. I mean, what is happiness? It's just so elusive."

"Why do you say that? Aren't you happy?"

"Of course I am," she said.

"Then you must know what it is."

In the silence that followed I listened to the measured tick of the mantle clock in the living room, an indication of how quiet our house had become. After a while I pondered aloud, "I wonder if they've done it yet."

"Done what?"

"Done . . . you know."

"Had sex?"

"Yeah."

"You mean Gwyn and Brandon?"

"Yeah."

"I don't think that's any of your business."

"I know. I was just wondering."

"That's disgusting."

"I know. It's just that, tomorrow is their wedding night and everything. I guess that just made me wonder about it."

"Well, don't."

"Why? It's not hurting anything."

"And don't you dare ask them anything like that tomorrow."

"I wouldn't do that."

"Don't ever ask them."

"I said I won't."

"If you ever ask them anything like that . . . .."

Attaching herself mysteriously to the conversation came a woman wearing a shimmery cocktail dress, sitting with me inside a posh bar, offering me samples of flavored Scotch. One after another she handed me little paper medicine cups filled with chocolate Scotch, watermelon Scotch, even, inexplicably, rum-flavored Scotch. They were promotional samples and she was a cute young kid just out of school with a marketing degree and I was wondering how to break it to her without hurting her feelings that the booze tasted just awful. I decided it would be easiest not to say anything at all about the Scotch, but to merely thank her and excuse myself and back gracefully away, but when I tried to speak my tongue felt unaccountably thick and awkwardly swollen and I couldn't make any words come out. I wondered how many samples I had drunk, and I looked to my left to plead to Anne to help me escape the situation when I realized that Anne wasn't there beside me after all, she was in the bathroom just finishing her A.M. shower. That could only mean that I wasn't in a posh bar at all and that there really was no such new product as flavored Scotch. I shook my head to clear away the remnants of the dream, but I stayed on the pillow with my eyes held open to focus. This was the wedding day. Looking at the alarm clock I was surprised to see how late I'd slept: going on eight o'clock.

"Why didn't you wake me up?" I said to Anne as she came from the bathroom.

"Why?" she answered. "You're not going to the breakfast. You don't have to be anywhere until one o'clock."

"I know. It's just that, I thought maybe you can use some help getting ready."

"I don't need any help," she said.

The breakfast was for the bridal party only, a champagned, catered affair hosted by Brandon's mother to brace the women for their hours-long ordeal involving makeup and hair. The wedding ceremony itself was scheduled to kick off at one at the big Presbyterian church with the massive, red wooden doors, a double set that opened to a view of the hedge-lined drive to the country club across the street, which was where the reception would be.

"I think you were just horrible last night," Anne shot at me, slicing through the mist and befuddlement that lingered still from the dream.

"Horrible? Last night? When? During dinner?"

"Not at dinner. Here. In bed. When we were talking."

"I was horrible?"

"Those things you said about Brandon and Gwyn."

"What did I say?"

"About Gwyn marrying Brandon for his money. And about whether they've been sleeping together yet."

"I didn't say she was marrying him for his money."

"You know how important today is to me. I don't want you doing anything or saying anything that's going to embarrass us."

"Why would I do that?"

"Because sometimes you do. But you'd better not. Not today. It's very important that Brandon gets a good impression of everybody."

"He's not marrying everybody. He's marrying Gwyn, and I would think he already has a good impression of her."

"You see: now you're starting again."

"I'm not starting. I just don't see why you're so worried about me saying something. I don't see why you're so worried about this wedding. It'll be fine. They've certainly spent enough."

The doorbell rang. Anne swung around at the sound. "Who the hell could that be," she said.

"It must be your ride."

"I'm not waiting for a ride. In fact, I'm supposed to be picking Gwyn up in about ten minutes. See how late you've made me. You'd better get that."

"It must be the paper boy."

"He's early."

"How much do we owe him?"

"I don't know. Give him a five."

I opened the front door thinking, what the hell, this wouldn't be the first time the paper boy saw me in my bathrobe, even though it was a rather heavy robe to be wearing on such a clear and warm May morning. But it was the only thing at hand to cover up with. I should buy some summer-weight bed clothes, I was thinking, when swinging open the door my eyes caught first on the tattered backpack lying on the stoop. Tracing up I saw Trevor Winkle standing here in front of me.

"I'm not staying here," he blurted, answering the question I must have posed by the shocked, startled, dumbfounded expression drawn over my face.

"You better believe you're not staying here," I said.

"I'm going to Pete and Elizabeth's. To your parents'. Only my mother wouldn't take me there. I wanted her to but she wouldn't. She said she didn't know them. She said she'd already called you and you were expecting me."

"She called here?"

"That's what she said."

"And you believed her?"

"No," he answered, and instantly, through my surprise, I felt sorry for the boy.

"Damn her," I pounded. "She just dropped you off again, didn't she? For how long?"

"Like, for the weekend."

"Where's she going this time?"

"I don't know."

"Doesn't she know anyone else you can stay with?"

"I'm going to Pete and Elizabeth's. Right away. But she said if I just went there and no one was home the neighbors might call the police or something. That's why I came here first. Can you, like, just call them or something to make sure they're home? I can get there on my own."

"How are you going to get there on your own?"

"I can hitchhike. I do it all the time. I do."

The kid looked every one of his fourteen years, and not a day older. I doubted if he had ever hitched a mile.

"This is ridiculous," I scoffed. "I can't believe she did this again. You can't hitchhike there. You couldn't even find the place from here. Go over there and wait by the garage. Over on the side where you're out of sight. No, wait—where'd she drop you off? Down at the corner again? Go back and wait there. I'll be by with the car in five minutes."

I watched through the open door until he got to the end of the driveway, to make sure he turned in the right direction. Anne was leaving any second but she wouldn't see him down at the corner because she'd be driving out the other way. With Trevor waiting down there she'd never see him. She'd never suspect a thing. But I should have taken a minute or two longer to calm and compose myself before rushing back to the bedroom to dress. Instead my head was fumbling to reorganize my morning: should I shave and shower now, or would I have time for all that when I got back? Should I call my parents just in case, to make sure they're home? I'd have plenty of time to shower when I got back if I didn't stay there too long. Of course they'll be home. They never went anywhere. But sometimes they went grocery shopping. If I showered now I'd have time to wait for them in case they were gone. But they wouldn't go this early, and it would take me too long to shower now.

"What's the matter," Anne quizzed me.

"Nothing."

"Then why are you rushing around?"

"I'm not."

"Who was that at the door?" But she already knew the answer and didn't need to wait for me, which was just as well, because I probably wouldn't have told her anyway.

"If that was Trevor Winkle at the door . . . Oh my God. It was, wasn't it? Trevor Winkle is here right now. He's standing in our living room this very second, isn't he? Isn't he?"

"No, he isn't."

"Then who was it?"

"I sent him away."

"Then where are you going?"

"I have to go take care of something. That's all. I'll be right back."

"You see." She sat down on the bed with a defeated air. "This is just what I've been talking about. Just when you think you have everything all worked out and that you're in the clear and that nothing can possibly go wrong . . . I told you that I didn't want you to do anything that was going to spoil things."

"I'm not doing anything. I'm going to get rid of him. Right away."

"How? Where? You're not bringing him to the wedding. And what am I supposed to do? The matron of honor is supposed to go to her sister's wedding without her husband? How in the hell does that make me look?"

"I'll be at the wedding."

"I just knew you'd pull something like this."

"I didn't pull anything. His mother just dropped him off again. I had no idea. I can get rid of him. I don't have anything else to do this morning anyway. I can get rid of him and get back here and have plenty of time to get dressed."

"He's not staying here," she insisted.

"I said I'm getting rid of him."

"Now my husband is going to miss my sister's wedding. I just knew something like this was going to happen."

"I won't miss the wedding. I have plenty of time."

"I wish I could believe that."

"Believe it."

She didn't have much choice. She looked at the clock on the night table. She was really late now.

"I really have to go," she said. "Okay, listen, at one o'clock, when I walk down that aisle ahead of Gwyn, I'd better see you sitting in that second pew."

"I'll be there," I told her.

Anne hastily gathered up her make-up bag and the suitcase stuffed with accessories and who knows what. She snatched up her gown hung on a hanger and draped in a long plastic bag.

"I'll be there long before one," I assured her.

"You'd better be," she said out the bedroom door. I listened to her footsteps clomping hastily down the stairs and across the kitchen floor. I heard her bang out into the garage. I rushed to a front window to watch her car back out. Anne swung the auto into the street and pointed it toward Gwyn's. I ran to the garage myself.

CHAPTER SEVEN

A second disaster waited for me that morning at my parents' home. An early hint of the trouble to greet me there came from Glen Watts, the deranged and belligerent neighbor. He was sweeping his driveway down near the road when Trevor and I rolled past. Watts had a small and shabby house that he did very little to care for. But he had a few neat-nick fetishes, like his compulsive raking. Another was sweeping his driveway. Mostly he pushed the broom as a pretense to be out front and be well positioned to crane and spy and intimidate. This morning he plied his broom with slow distraction as he stared intensely at my parents' house.

I swung the car anxiously into Peter and Elizabeth's driveway, just in time to see a fat brown book cascade from an upstairs window and whump onto the ground. I sprung swiftly out of the auto and arched to look up at the house. The window above me was broken out edge to edge, with both the top pane and bottom pane cleared of glass so that only jagged, glinting shards remained at the frame. The broken glass lay in angular bits on the ground right below it. All the windows I could see on the bottom floor were smashed out the same way, cleared crudely of glass that littered the outside ground beneath them, leaving blank, dark holes that opened into the house like wounds. Possessions like the book disgorged from the house lay everywhere on the ground surrounding it and hung up on the shrubs that encircled the building. A flurry of papers and some unopened mail. An electric mixer from the kitchen. A set of plastic soup bowls and some pans. A calendar. A fork. The little basket my parents kept near the phone. The telephone itself – not quite on the ground but dangling out against the chalking wooden clapboard, still tethered by its cord to the plug inside. Whole armsful of clothing. Towels. A toothbrush. A shoe. A small footstool. Two candlesticks. As I gaped another brown volume hurtled down from the second-floor window. Like the first book, it was from the big Britannica set my parents had bought years back, for assignments and homework when I was a kid in school.

I arched up again in time to see the blunt end of a broomstick jab through another window above me. It butted the glass again and again rapidly from inside the house until the entire pane was pushed out in jangling pieces. Then the broomstick scoured franticly around the window frame to flake away the larger points of glass that still clung at the edges.

I stared up amazed, unable to speak and unable even to comprehend the scene that I saw. As I watched, the methodical broomstick pierced the window's top pane and cleared all the glass from that frame too.

At last I hollered up, "hey, what are you doing? What in the hell are you doing up there?"

My father's face appeared in the broken-out window. He looked down at me surprised, not comprehending. His eyes were wide and darting, enflamed. He panted and heaved.

"Dad, did you do all this," I shouted up at him. "What in the hell are you doing? Did you throw all this stuff out here?"

"I'm getting rid of it all," he pounced back. "I'm getting rid of everything. I don't want it anymore. I'm getting rid of it. Everything. This whole damn house. I can't keep up with it anymore. They can have it all."

"You broke all these windows?" I asked in amazement.

"I don't want it anymore," he yelled down. His head pulled in.

"Want what," I shouted.

His head popped out again. "All this," he yelled back. "Everything. I don't want it. I can't take care of it anymore. I can't keep up with it."

"Why in the hell did you break all these windows," I scolded.

He looked side to side, as if he could see the whole scene from inside the room where he stood.

"Who in the hell's gonna fix all this," I shouted.

"Nobody," he yelled. "I don't want it fixed. I want the rain the come in. The wind and snow. The birds and the bugs. They can have it all. I can't live here anymore." He started to duck inside again.

"Wait a second," I shouted. "What in the hell are you doing?"

"I'm giving it back," he replied. He looked enlarged. Engorged. Possessed.

"Giving what back?"

"Everything. The house. The clothes. Everything."

"What are you talking about?"

"I said I don't want it anymore. Let the wind and the rain come in. I'm too damn tired of keeping 'em out."

He disappeared inside.

I ran to the nearest door, the side door next to the driveway. But I couldn't get in because the outside aluminum storm door was pried partially away from the doorjamb, yanked loose metal frame and all so that the wood of the doorjamb was splintered where screws had pulled out. The aluminum door was left kinked and twisted and wedged in the opening so that I couldn't snake past it. Inside I saw the heavier, wooden inner door lying askew on the floor where it had fallen after Peter had popped out its hinge pins. I ran around to the front door, stepping over debris from the house as I raced. A kleenex box. A table lamp. Crossword book. A pillow from the couch. Framed photos. Coffee mug. Support hose. Alarm clock. A bag of Doritos. Stapler. Trevor had popped out of the car and he was pacing quickly to join me.

"You get back in that car," I shouted at him. "You get in there and stay there and don't come out."

I found the front door the same as the side, with the main wooden door slammed inward onto the floor with its hinge pins removed, the outer, aluminum storm door pried away at the frame. But this time I could wedge open the metal door far enough to slip past it and step inside. I stepped over a crowbar that Peter had left abandoned there, fetched up from a heap of tools in the basement and used to tug loose the storm doors – or tug them partially loose before he quit and rushed off to savage the windows. From inside the house I heard another one break. I charged up the stairs. I found my father in a bedroom.

"What in the hell are you doing," I scolded.

He turned to glare at me. His eyes flamed. Both his hands gripped the handle of a hard-sided suitcase. He twisted and wound up to swing it with fury against an unbroken window. But I reached him in time and locked both my arms around him before he could spin the suitcase through the pane. I tugged him across the floor until we were safely away from the unbroken window. I pried his tenacious hands from the suitcase handle.

"What in the hell are you doing," I repeated.

"It's no use," he said as his breath heaved out and in and out and in. He struggled to fit in the words between gasps. "I can't do it anymore," he wheezed. "There's no use trying. The weather can take it all. Take the whole damn place. I can't stop it now anyway."

"Are you crazy," I said.

"It'll all be gone in a year," he said. "This whole damn place. That's all it will take. A year. Just wait till the rain comes in. Then all the animals. The plants will start. Their roots. Wait till wintertime."

"How are we going cleaned up this mess," I demanded.

We looked around the room. Peter was silent at last. We both stared at the mess. He had thrown clothing in heaps on the floor from the closet. He had pulled drawers from a dresser and dumped them. Dresses and blouses and socks and skirts and slips and brassieres: my mother's things.

"Where's mom," I asked him. But Peter merely blinked back at me blankly. His breath snapped in and flicked out, snapped in and flicked out, growing softer each time, as if he was deflating notch by notch.

"You follow me now," I commanded. "You stay right behind me and don't you dare go anyplace else."

With father in tow, docile now, I found Elizabeth standing in the kitchen. She bent at the waist awkwardly, he feet splayed and her balance uncertain, picking up glass from the floor near a window. She straightened like rusted machinery and carried the small handful of glass to the trash can beneath the sink.

"She's going to cut herself again," father said vacantly, as if he was speaking to himself.

"Mom, are you all right," I asked her.

"Make her sit down," Peter said. "She's going to cut herself on that glass." He stepped to the kitchen table and sat down himself. His fire now was completely extinguished. He looked bloodless. His expression showed only vague terror.

But Elizabeth was serene. She most likely did not remember Peter's destructive rampage, now just a moment after I'd stopped it, the ruckus erased by her Alzheimer's. She went to the table and picked up two plates left there from breakfast. She carried them to the sink and began to run water, to wash them with the few bits of kitchen ware lingering there. She guarded her right hand, carrying it cautiously. I stepped nearer and saw a red gash across her palm.

"Ma, what happened to your hand?"

She looked down, gazing first at the back of her hand. When she rolled it palm upward she saw the blood seeping and intermingling with the water that clung from the sink.

"Oh, look at that," she said. "I don't know what happened to it. I must have done something to hurt it somehow. I don't know what I did to myself this time."

I lifted her hand and wiped away soap suds. The cut ran about an inch across her palm, but it was not deep. The blood oozed very slowly, coloring to pink in the water that pooled in her palm's upward cup.

"You shouldn't be doing the dishes," I said. "Doesn't it hurt?"

"Hurt? No. It's a little bit painful. But I can still move it just fine."

To my father across the room at the table I asked, "dad, what did mom do to her hand?"

"She broke through a window."

"A window? You mean one of these windows you smashed?"

"No. Before that. She was up on the stool washing it. I think that's what she was doing. I think she slipped and she put her hand out and it went right through the window."

"Why was she washing a window?"

"I don't know why."

"Weren't you watching her?"

"I was reading the paper in the chair in there. She was right there with me. I must have fallen asleep. It was just for a few minutes. I didn't know she was doing anything. Then I heard the window break."

"You know you have to watch her," I said. "You can't fall asleep when she's awake. You knew something like this could happen. Or she could wander off and get lost or something. We've talked about this."

"I can't watch her every second. I just can't keep up anymore. The windows were dirty."

"She could have hurt herself a lot worse than this."

"I can't do it anymore."

"And why did you get so mad about it? Why did you bust out every window in the whole damn house? Why'd you throw

JEFFREY ZYGMONT

all your stuff outside? What are we supposed to do now? I'm supposed to be at a wedding in a little while. If you'd been watching her in the first place none of this would have happened."

"I can't watch her every second. It's just too much. It's just . . . I'm . . . I'll . . . aurgh." His voice trailed into incomprehension.

"At least it's not a bad cut," I said mostly to console myself. "It's really just a scratch. It's a little bit deep for a scratch, but I still wouldn't call it a cut. You're barely bleeding at all, mom. I can bandage it up with some gauze. But you shouldn't use it for a few days till it heals. Dad, you'll have to watch her to make sure she takes it easy with this hand."

"She should go to the hospital," Peter intoned

"You're not putting me away in any hospital," Elizabeth protested.

"That's just what she said before," Peter said.

"Is that what started all this," I asked, sweeping my arm to encompass the wrecking-ball damage surrounding us.

"She needs to have that looked at but she won't let me take her. She fights me about everything. I can't get anything done anymore. I just can't keep up with it."

"Her hand is all right," I said. It had to be all right. I didn't have time to fit in an emergency room visit too. I had already stayed longer than I ever intended. I had the wedding. Anne waiting. I surveyed the damage around me. Smashed out windows. The door slammed onto the floor. Strewn pots and cooking pans scattered. Others disgorged to the ground outside. A drawer of essential utensils flipped onto the floor – spud masher, spatula, whisk, garlic press, pastry brush, corer, jar opener, wine screw, skewers, meat hammer, tea ball, carving fork, tongs.

And this was just the kitchen. I would need hours to put the house in any kind of order.

"I don't think she needs stitches," I said in consolation again. "All a doctor will do is bandage her up and tell her to stay off the hand. We can do that ourselves right here."

"I can't do anything anymore," moaned my father.

The aluminum door at the side of the house, the one I had failed to tug open, made a grating, rasping yelp and screeched loudly as Trevor yanked it outward a gap and stepped inside. He stayed at the edge of the kitchen, not quite among us.

"I told you to stay in the car," I said.

"He can't stay here," Peter said, his voice rising a tone as alarm and agitation returned.

"What are you going to do," Trevor asked me.

"I don't know. I guess I'll clean up. What else can I do. I'll need your help. We don't have much time."

"Okay," Trevor said.

"I can't have anyone staying here now," Peter went on.

I acknowledged to myself that I could never make it to the church in time for the wedding. But if I hustled enough, with Trevor's help, I could still make the reception and dinner after the wedding. That would be my opportunity to explain, to make amends and patch up the inevitable rift with Anne, my wife.

We started with all the indoor goods that Peter had flung through the windows. Trevor and I gathered the debris in heaping armsful that we carried back into the house, tumbling it into chock-a-block piles wherever we found room, on chairs and tables and out of the way on the floor. Below all the windows outside we picked up only the larger chunks of glass that we could manage by hand. But inside we swept the slivers and splinters into a dustpan and sloughed the mess into a trash can that grew heavy from the load. From his stay here the weekend before, Trevor knew where to find the vacuum, which he used to suck up the fine powder and pulverized glass that remained on the floor. We picked up the litter from the floors of the primary rooms, the rooms that my parents used regularly, just dropping the clothing into closets and stuffing objects hastily back into drawers that Peter had overturned. Yanking together in unison, we pulled the gnarled storm doors wide and left them stuck open from their strenuous warping. We hefted the inner doors back into place and I held them in their frames while Trevor tapped in the hinge pins with a hammer he'd fetched from the basement. The best we could do for the shattered windows was to tack coverings over the holes. We used bed-sheets and towels from the bathroom. We finished in the kitch-en, where Peter and Elizabeth now sat silently at the table. We stuffed pots and plates into cupboards and dropped the spatula, pastry brush, meat hammer and all the rest into drawers, tidying the room enough to make it maneuverable at least. I hoped that my mother and father would also find it usable until I could return to make more effective repairs.

"I have to leave now," I told them. "Anne's sister's wedding is today. Remember. I told you. I'm already too late for the ceremony. But if I get home now and get ready I can make it to the reception at least. I don't want to miss that too."

Peter began fidgeting and fussing again at the table.

"But he can't stay here," he said to me. "Not again. I can't have anyone stay here when the place is like this."

I looked over at Trevor.

"But I can help you clean it up more," Trevor said to my father. "Like last week. Remember how much I did last week? You said that I helped you catch up."

"Look at this place," my father said to me alone. His agitation was visibly rising. "It's a mess here. The place is a shambles. There's not any windows. There's not a room he can sleep in. He can't stay here this time."

"But that's just what he said last time," Trevor pleaded to me. "Just last weekend he said exactly the same thing. Remember? He said I couldn't stay here but you said I had to. And we did just fine. I finished cutting the grass and then I did a whole bunch of other things till you picked me up here on Sunday. Remember? And that started out the same way. Pete said I couldn't stay here but after I did, then it was fine."

"There's not even a room," father said to me with weary insistence. "Not even a bed. I have too much to do already. There's just too much. I can't keep up with it anymore."

"But I can help you again," Trevor insisted. "Just like the last time. Remember? I can pick up some more. I'll have lots of time to pick up and put everything away better this time. I can fix things. Just like the last time. You didn't want me to stay then, either. But after you were glad."

"No," father said. His chest started to heave again. "I don't even have a room for him. They're all wrecked."

"I don't care if I don't have a room," Trevor insisted. "I stay lots of places where I don't have a room. Or a bed or even a couch sometimes."

Peter's eyes darted and dodged. He scanned the room in bursts. He shot furtive glances at me. At Trevor. His jaw drooped sullenly. He grimaced. He twisted his hands and flicked his fingers. He reached beneath the table and rubbed his palms against his thighs. He stood up abruptly and strode to a window. He shuddered with surprise to find a towel tacked across its raw opening, having forgotten his own rampage from barely a couple of hours before. He grimaced and heaved a few breaths. He wandered back to the table but stayed on his feet, staring vacantly into the home's interior. He was so far imbalanced that I could not risk leaving the boy here. It might tip him still further. I would have to keep Trevor with me, which meant taking him along to the wedding reception.

CHAPTER EIGHT

I put Trevor in an old suit that had gone so snug on me that I could scarcely button the jacket or snap up the pants. Naturally it was too large for him. I couldn't do anything about the coat, which sagged around him like the husk on a desiccated bean. I rolled up the pants a turn on the bottom to fix the length, smoothing the folds to make them look like actual cuffs. They still looked like rolled up pants, which was all right because that way they might at least divert some attention from his shoes, which were actually my father's shoes, a pair he had flung out a broken window and that I, showing uncharacteristic foresight, had tossed into my car when Trevor and I were picking up. They fit the boy, but that was the best that could be said about them. They were tired old wingtips with scuffed wide soles that had broken down across the toes from too much wear. I thought they might flap when he walked, and I wondered if Trevor would refuse to come with me altogether, looking the way he did. But I told him that this was how dressy clothes were worn today. He bought it, not having any experience with neckties that might disprove my claim.

Besides, it turned out that I was right, though unwittingly. When we arrived at the reception Trevor blended right in with a clubby knot of nephews and nieces and other elevated urchins from the extended family of the groom. They had dressed down, putting on shabbiness, nonchalance and a general youthful disdain for any authority that might be expressed in conventional attire. Or maybe it was more an affluent disdain, because although their ensembles were a discordant mishmash of styles, every piece of their clothing smelled of boutique cash. And at second glance their outfits weren't exactly haphazard, either. They were calculated, from the narrow straight-edge ties to the wide-lapelled, padded-up zoots to the, yes, wing-tipped brogues. But so what if this was the mere affectation of poverty, which country-club kids put on with such careful élan. I nonetheless felt grateful that Trevor's baggy, beau-jangles pants and his jacket that looked like a towel thrown over a post didn't stand out as much as I had originally feared.

We arrived just a minute too late to march through the receiving line with the rest of the guests. I was sorry for that, because I had imagined that its stiff formality and its ritual handshakes and hugs would give me a welcomed opportunity to greet Anne inside a structured setting, and in the company of witnesses, to re-introduce myself, in a way, and maybe to at least start my explanation of why I had missed her sister's wedding ceremony, and why I had now brought the orphaned boy along to the reception, and why I'd done the half-dozen or so other things she had told me, expressly, just that morning, not to do. If I gave her at least the rough outline while she stood in the receiving line, as I had hoped, Anne wouldn't be able to break ranks to assail me. She'd be forced to hear it all. Maybe that would buy more time for my explanations to sink in.

But when Trevor and I walked in the bridal party had just retired to the terrace, for photographs, perhaps, or maybe just to breath some gusts of the fragrant May air. I cut to the bar, eager to fortify myself. I had at least a few chaotic moments left before people sat down to dinner. I felt securely inconspicuous amid the fluid little mobs of folks clustered near the bar and in front of the head table, milling beside the wedding cake, the gift table, and along walls and in corners throughout the room. Trevor stayed at my heel. When we reached the bar the down-dressed rich kids were there, three of them huddled into a dark recess near the wall. With determined nonchalance they glanced side-long at Trevor, sizing him. Trevor did the same, taking in the group in a single, furtive glance meant to be unnoticed, or to convey coolly that he hadn't noticed them. In their corner the three teens closed the incident by bowing their heads to sip silently from the colas they held in their hands.

"It's an open bar," I said to Trevor. "Why don't you get yourself a soda or something?"

"Open?"

"It means it's free. All you do is go up and tell the bartender what you want."

"Oh. I know."

"Don't you want anything?"

"I'm not thirsty right now."

I wanted him to get something simply because I didn't know what else to do with him, and because I already felt too conspicuous. We might look more at ease, I reasoned, if we each held a glass in our hand. Defeated, I bellied up without him, flipping the remark, "Well I'm going to get something." And repeating, "You sure you don't want me to get something for you?"

"I'm all right," he shrugged.

So I ventured the last three steps alone, shouldering through the tight press of people, the loud crowd, who wanted as desperately as I did to hover on the lip of the bar. I knew a lot of them, of course, since at least half the wedding guests had to be my relatives-in-law. Therefore I didn't look directly at anyone. I watched impatiently as the barman poured a whorl of red wine into the generously rounded glass. I just got it to my lips when a pre-emptive slap on my back jarred the glass away from me, causing me to spill a viscous dollop onto the bar. I stretched a look over my shoulder to see who I had to thank for the rude greeting. It was Roger, who was married to Rita, the middle sister of Anne, my wife.

"Where have you been," Roger grinned. "We were saving a seat for you in church. What'd you do? Sit in the back?"

"Yeah. Well, actually, I didn't make it."

"Whoa. Ducked out of the ceremony, eh? I wouldn't of minded if I missed it myself. How'd you manage to get away with it?"

"I didn't. I mean, I was supposed to be there. There was an emergency."

"An emergency?"

Rita pushed her way through to us.

"Boy, is my sister ever mad at you," she told me.

"I had to go to my parents' house," I said to them. "It was completely unexpected. You know how my mother's been doing. And my father too. This morning they had sort of an accident."

"An accident," said Roger. "I hope everyone's all right."

"You'd better tell Anne," Rita said. "It's a good thing you have a good excuse. She doesn't know where you've been."

"It's all right now," I said. "I had to stay and put everything back together. My father had sort of a, well, I guess you could call it a fit."

"What do you mean by a fit," asked Roger. Rita stepped in closer and canted her head to the side to lock in on my response. Clearly she was hungry for some serious conversation. Or maybe she just wanted to see if my excuse would measure up.

"He's been kind of depressed lately. You know: my mother's condition has really got to him."

"So, what happened?"

"She hurt her hand this morning. It's nothing very serious, but it was enough to send him over the deep end."

"What did he do?"

"He kind of wrecked the place."

"Like what?"

"He smashed out all the windows."

"All of them?" asked Rita.

"Almost all. There were two upstairs that he didn't get to. I stopped him just in time. Who knows what else he would have done if I didn't get there when I did." I lathered on the melodrama, to help assure that my excuse would indeed measure up. Rita and Anne were close sisters, and I was certain they'd talk.

"Wow," Rita marveled. "It sounds like he really did lose it. You'd better tell Anne. She was ready to kill you a little while ago."

"Where are they?"

"I don't know. They're over there someplace. Everybody is getting ready to sit down now."

"How much do you think it costs to join this place?" asked Roger.

"I don't know. I'm sure it costs a lot."

"I haven't seen any black members yet," he joked.

"I don't like country clubs," said Rita.

"I can't believe people pay all this money just to have a place to play golf," Roger said.

"It's not just for golf," Rita said. "Look at this place. It's more of a social thing."

I looked, but only to see over the heads of the people huddled around the bar to find Trevor. Where in the hell had he gone?

"I have to go find someone," I announced abruptly to Rita and Roger.

"Anne's up there by the head table," Rita advised. "Everybody's getting ready to sit down now."

"We're all sitting up there anyway," Roger told me. "There's a family table right by the head table. It's got all our name cards on it."

"Name cards?"

"That's right. Assigned seats."

"Damn it," I said. "I'm going to need an extra seat."

"For who?"

"You'd better go see Anne," Rita advised. "A minute ago she was ready to kill you. I bet she still is."

I pushed out to where I had left the boy. He was there, near the same spot, at least, and I felt an instant rush of relief. One of the down-dressed kids had broken off from her group and was talking to him. She was a heavy girl, a bit older than Trevor. She wore a black leather skirt that showed off short, thick legs that still retained the firm tone of her youth. As I stepped beside

Trevor the two of them clammed up. It didn't look like they had been having much of a conversation, anyway.

"Is this your father?" she asked him.

"No."

She looked me up and down.

"I'm his guardian," I told her.

"As in 'legal guardian,' as in 'parent or legal guardian' on all those school forms?"

"Sort of," I said. "This time it's a little more temporary than that."

"That's a new one," she said to Trevor, disregarding me. "'Parent or temporary legal guardian.'"

The bar crowd had begun to migrate like a scattering herd toward the dining tables. For a moment I resisted its tug. I stood on my toes and peered to find the table reserved for family members up near the head table. I wondered where I was going to find another seat. It had never occurred to me that the table settings would be reserved. I had planned to simply sit inconspicuously in the back with the boy.

"Time to go," said Roger, appearing at my elbow with Rita. "Here," he said, "I already got you another glass of wine."

"I need to find another seat for someone," I said.

"Relax. Rita already took care of it."

"You did?"

"I grabbed a waiter and told him to set another place at our table," Rita explained. "It's going to be kind of tight. Who is he?"

Rita, Roger and I turned together to look at Trevor, still there at my elbow with the girl. I readied my tongue to say guardian. How much did I want to explain, I wondered.

"Do you want a drink or not," the big girl asked Trevor.

"I don't know."

"Come on," she said. She led him to the bar, now pretty much clear of people.

"We'll be up front," Rita called to him. "We've got a seat for you up there." Then she asked me again, "Who is he?"

"It's kind of a long story. He's from the school. It's one of these mixed up family situations."

"He looks like a hard-luck case," she said. "I thought maybe it was one of those 'Big Brother, Big Sister of America' arrangements."

"I thought maybe he was your son," Roger laughed.

"Isn't that your old suit he's wearing?"

"I don't have a son."

I walked between them to our table. Everyone else in the room was seated by now, so we stood out. Anne wasn't looking at me—purposefully not looking. I could see that she was seething. She leaned forward over the long head table to look across Gwyn and Brandon, bride and groom, to watch the best man on their other side, who was tapping his empty cup to bring the room to attention. He motioned for us to stand for the toast. The whole room erupted cheerfully, vertically, just as the waiters retracted hastily from each table, having filled the last of the champagne glasses. Roger, Rita and I reached our seats amid this tumult. I looked back. I couldn't see through the crowd to where we had left Trevor. Above us the best man tapped insistently, gaily. I gulped. I turned. For the first time I faced the head table head on. Anne wasn't looking at me. I didn't look at her. Mercifully, we both had the best man to focus on, as he tapped merrily to quiet us rumbling guests.

"It's time to get started," he said. "If I could have everyone's attention, please." He looked quite at ease with leadership.

"It's time to begin," he said again. "Gwendolyn, Brandon,

will you please stand up here with me."

They rose together, bride and groom, hand held in hand, looking radiantly out across the room. There must have been three hundred of us gazing back at them, our elbows cocked for the toast. We held the champagne in slender stemmed glasses that fizzed.

"I have to admit, there was a time when I thought it would never come to this," began the best man. "Brandon was as confirmed a bachelor as any man I have ever known. I won't go into all the details, Gwyn." (The room tittered with laughter.) "But it speaks rather well of you—and especially of the relationship that the two of you share—that here you stand together, having just exchanged vows, and now ready to enjoy your first meal together as husband and wife, with all of us here as witnesses to share in your happiness." A buzz of approval arose. He'd rehearsed this. Not that he needed rehearsal. He belonged to the select caste whose members actually wear tuxedos as well and as comfortably as the go-to-work multitudes feel wearing sweat suits. But how could he help it? His tuxedo wasn't rental clothing. The best man, and the groom too, I imagined, owned these black-tie attires and probably a couple of other such suits besides, for variety's sake, because as members of this club and probably some other, similar establishments, they would find many occasions fit for formal wear.

"I don't intend to drag this out too long," continued the best, "because I can see Chef Suzi standing in the back. She only comes out of the kitchen when she's impatient to get dinner out onto the tables. And, believe me, we don't want to wait any longer for the wonderful meal that she's prepared. (More laughter and approving clatter.) So let's begin with a simple toast." He raised his glass dramatically. "Gwendolyn and Brandon.

May this be only the first of a lifetime of sumptuous meals shared with each other, and, occasionally, with we friends."

I slammed down the drink in a single head toss. I turned and looked toward the bar again, hoping to spot Trevor picking his way here among the well-wishers. Where was he? It was impossible to see anything with everyone standing and slurping champagne. I made a quick and desperate break for the back of the room. The guests began to sit in a noisy, jumbling, rumbling mass. I tried to go even faster but hooked my foot in the leg of a chair. I stumbled, nearly fell, and had to lurch and scurry for a few steps to regain my balance. By the time I pulled up awkwardly from the dive everyone else was seated—everyone except me. I stood conspicuously in the center of the hall, alone among all the tables and chairs filled with eager-to-eat merry makers. The white-coated waiters pushed out of the kitchen carrying big trays stacked with wide white bowls. They fanned out at the tables to set the bowls, deferentially, one at a time, beneath the nose of each guest. There'd be soup to start. I peered over the crowd toward the back of the room. There he was, sitting at a table with a handful of other kids. The three down-dressed teens were there, along with a couple others of their ilk, and a few younger children too, tossed together as a hodge-podge of near peers. Every one of them was watching Trevor, wide grins on their faces. He was showboating, clowning, miraculously in his element. That was the most I could make out. I dared not stand any longer. I satisfied myself with the fact that he was settled there for the meal. Better there, I thought, in a far, dark corner, than up with me under Anne's glare. How much mischief could he make? The kids would keep their wisecracks to themselves, and hold themselves aloof from us adults as they watched us play at our own buffoonery outside the margin of their little enclave.

I made my way back to my own table, wishing I was smaller. Anne still wasn't looking at me. I slipped into my seat just as a pair of waiters arrived at the table. One carried a big silver tureen, which, he announced, was potato-leek soup, which is peasant fare gone tony, though that wasn't announced. His companion, the assistant waiter, ladled portions into our bowls, beginning with the ladies, of course. They stopped at the place on my left, the empty seat that had been set for Trevor.

"We won't be needing that anymore," I said up at them. "I mean, there won't be anyone sitting here after all."

"Where is he?" Rita quizzed me from across the table. Roger sat next to her, and beside him was Anne's brother, plus another sister, both with their spouses. On the other side of Rita, opposite Roger, sat another of Anne's sisters, Anita, who was the youngest next to Gwyn, the bride. Anita was also with her husband, and next to him—across the gap left at Trevor's place—sat his daughter, a girl of seventeen or so from his first marriage, the husband being noticeably older than Anne's sister Anita, whom he'd married only about a year earlier. The daughter, Stephanie, was a precocious girl. She could have passed easily for a sister next to Anita, her stepmother. Except that the teen still hadn't developed a comfortable social bearing, remaining still in the nether land between girl and woman, which caused her to sit quietly ill-at-ease among us. I think the lavish luxury of the hall unnerved her a little too. She was unaccustomed to it, though she recognized well enough that her set of everyday social rules might be inadequate here. She would need more, though she couldn't imagine what. The situation made her cow-eyed, and I wished for her that she could simply relax and enjoy, instead of watching the rest of us so carefully, noting every gesture, recording every word, so that she could discover from us how she herself should behave here. I doubted that she'd find a suitable model among us.

"Where is he?" quizzed Rita.

"Yeah, what happened to your son," Roger followed. I felt the swing of their eyes as my in-laws at the table turned to probe me. I wished he'd shut up. Anne wasn't that far away. I wondered if she could hear him.

"He's sitting in the back," I said, anxious to finish the answer. "He's not my son," I couldn't resist adding.

"What are you talking about," asked the eldest sister, Grace.

"Dan is a Big Brother," Rita answered for me. "Kind of. He brought a boy with him. That's why we needed the extra place."

"It's the son we never knew he had," quipped Roger again.

"Why doesn't he already have a seat? Isn't he on the guest list," asked the sister. I felt their eyes swing back at me. Stephanie in particular, the near-adult daughter, ill at ease, looked across the empty seat to regard me with sudden interest, her bovine eyes going a notch wider. She had to be wondering: could someone really just up and bring an uninvited guest to an affair like this?

"No, he wasn't invited," I answered.

"Don't you think that's kind of tacky," said Anita, drawing her step-daughter's eyes for an instant, but only for that, as Stephanie snapped her gaze back to me, eager for my response, eyes notched open even wider.

"It gets kind of complicated," I said. "I never planned to bring him. In fact, I never expected him to be around. In fact, I barely even know him. He has to do with work."

"Dan's had a pretty rough day," Rita volunteered. "Have

you explained anything to Anne yet?"

"Still, to just bring him here like that," said Anita. "Somebody has to pay for all this, you know."

"They look like they can afford it," Roger cracked.

"I think it's tacky."

"What happened to you today?" Anita's husband asked me, he being the elder at the table, making a gesture, perhaps, of apology for his wife's badgering.

"I don't want to get into it," I told them. "Let's just say that I had no choice. I wouldn't have brought him if I had had a choice. In fact, he's the last person I would have brought. But I didn't have a choice. So I brought him."

"I'm sure you could have found something else to do with him," Anita said.

"I don't see what the big deal is," dared callow young Stephanie, who just as quickly regretted her boldness. But it was too late to turn back, because now all eyes swung to her, in surprise as much as anything. "I mean, it's not like he's causing a problem or anything," she stammered on defensively. "We wouldn't even know he was here if we weren't all talking about him."

"Where is he, anyway," Rita asked me. "I still don't see him."

"Excuse us, but is anyone sitting here?" The voice interposed itself abruptly in the empty space next to me. It belonged to Alex, older brother of the groom. He presented a stunning blonde.

"This is Phyllis," he said. "There's been a little mix up and there's no room for her over at our table. I wonder if you'd mind if she sat here for dinner?"

Phyllis slid into the empty chair flashing a smile that, in

other circumstances, can get women into magazines. The step-daughter recoiled a little nervously, inching her chair closer to her father, away from Phyllis, as Phyllis settled into the seat between Stephanie and me.

"It's awfully nice of you," said Phyllis, looking Stephanie congenially square in the face as she addressed the table. "I hope you don't mind me butting in like this." A consensus of smiles and nods and "not at alls" came back at her. Phyllis's little dress, a black sheath, had no back. It was as good bet that, with Phyllis here, the men at the table would do very little talking.

"Did they forget to reserve a place for you," asked Rita.

"Well, not exactly. Technically, I'm not supposed to be here. Well, that's not exactly true, either. But Alex and I started seeing each other just a couple weeks ago. We've known each other for a really long time, but we only started going out after his divorce came through. That was after all of this was already put together. I mean the invitations and the guest list and everything." She shrugged her shoulders playfully. "Alex just forget to add me."

I noticed Anne up at the head table gazing down at me—at us. I didn't make eye contact.

"It's a good thing we had an extra spot," ventured step-daughter Stephanie.

"I know," Phyllis replied, shining a big grin on the young woman. "It's right next to Alex's table and everything. We thought I'd have to sit on the other side of the room or something." The two women nodded cheerful agreement. Stephanie no longer listed toward her father.

Even with Phyllis beside me, I spooned my soup bowl dry. I hadn't eaten a whiff of food all day, though I hadn't noticed my hunger until now, until the buttery, onion-cut aroma of the steaming potato mash wafted through my sinuses. When the assistant waiter returned to tong a salt-topped, crusty bread roll onto my side plate I caught it in my palm before it dropped. I tore it to chunks that fit just barely into my mouth. I handled the salad of colored kale and darkly leafed greens—with julienned strips of tender-crisp red and yellow peppers and drizzlings of oil-rich dressing—as if I was tossing hay with a pitchfork. I attacked the main course, thick medallions of beef tenderloin arranged like fallen dominoes on a wide white plate, seeping with steaming meat juice, sided by puffs of potatoes with a grating of pepper and a sprinkling of dill, sided again by white, slender spears of asparagus crosshatched with glistening sauce. I swigged down acrid red wine in gulps that pinched up into my nostrils. The assistant waiter, a square-cut kid who looked trim, fit and unaccountably nautical in his white jacket, came often to refill my glass. I called him Popeye in good humor, and he laughed and replenished my wine more attentively yet, with graver mock ceremony. Phyllis and Stephanie talked together brightly beside me. I ate without speaking, just dimly aware of their conversation circling around me. I left but a few saucy smudges on the generous plate. I forgot all about Trevor and Anne and the glowering look that Anne had shot at me, or at Phyllis, or at both of us.

The others were still at their food when at last I pushed back from my plate. Sated, I let the waft of conversation penetrate my thoughts. Phyllis and Stephanie carried most of it, with Phyllis quipping about how "God already made good food look good to us," and I remembered dully that they were talking about the chef's presentation, the careful arrangement of sides and sauces and the array of beef on each plate, which Phyllis, to my surprise, took for superfluous.

"I know," said Stephanie. "And you only have to mess it up to eat it, anyway." Which Stephanie did, spooning in a bite she plainly relished. I swilled down my last large gulp of grape pressings and Popeye appeared at attention at my elbow, eager for me to put down the glass. As he sloshed in another ample dram Phyllis looked up at him gaily and asked if he could find another plateful for me in the kitchen. He returned that he didn't think I liked the meal well enough and the whole table laughed. Assistant waiter Popeye laughed too and I reached for the new wine merrily.

"Now, I really hate to ask you this now," Phyllis addressed to the table. "I mean, I should have asked you sooner but I got carried away with the meal. Wasn't it great?"

"I never had food so good," beamed Stephanie.

"But, I can't remember any of your names. I know we just met at the church, so I really should remember. But I've always been so bad about names. Oh, I feel so stupid asking this now, after we've been talking together through this whole big meal."

Rita, who hadn't been talking through the whole meal, and who therefore seemed to have a pent up ambition to speak, took over. She introduced herself and husband Roger. She introduced her brother and sister on her left, dutifully naming each and their spouses. She nodded toward Anita on her right, and Anita's maturing husband too.

"And I'm Stephanie," shot in the step-daughter. "You wouldn't know that, because we didn't officially meet at the church. I get overlooked sometimes."

"And who are you?" asked Phyllis, turning and laying her hand lightly on my arm.

"That's Dan," said Rita.

"I don't think we met at the church either, did we, Dan?"

She reached across with her right, giving me just her fingers to grasp as we shook, returning a light pressure against my palm.

"He wasn't at the church," Rita said.

"Oh. So how could we have met? And what's your relation to everyone," Phyllis asked me.

"He's married to the matron of honor."

"Really," she beamed. "So you're Annie's husband. I thought maybe you were the black-sheep bachelor of the family or something."

"He is a black sheep," shot Stephanie, coloring a little afterward at her boldness.

"Your wife is so beautiful," Phyllis told me. She whacked my arm playfully, scolding, "Why didn't you come to see her in the wedding?"

"He got tied up," said Rita. "There was an emergency at his parents' house."

"And he had to bring his son," blurted Roger, his first words spoken since Phyllis arrived.

She squared toward me in her chair, laying her hands in her lap and opening wide her eyes in an attentive invitation, a signal that she was waiting for an explanation.

"We've been stuck on this all day," I said. "For the last time, he's not my son. I don't have a son. I don't have any children." I tossed down another big swig of wine. Popeye refilled my glass. "It's a long story," I said. "I'm sure you don't want to hear the whole thing. I have, well, let's call it temporary custody of a boy. A teenager, really. It's because of my work. I'm the psychologist for the schools here. He's having some, well, let's just say some family problems. I was supposed to leave him at my parents' today, to kind of baby-sit, but they couldn't. They've been having problems too. So I had to bring him along at the last minute. That's why I didn't make it to the church. I'm lucky I made it here in time."

"Where is he," asked Phyllis.

"He's sitting in the back with some other kids."

"I think that's so sweet," she said. "He's just like me: an uninvited guest."

The orchestra had been gradually, imperceptibly adding volume and intensity throughout the meal, until now it broke through just as the corps of waiters, ever dutiful, cleared the last lingering dessert plates, taking back sagging remnants of a creme brulee. Hastily I scraped a few smears of sauce off my plate with the side of a fork which I then sucked clean. The room lights came down as the music rose higher. The bridal party was due to dance the opener. I stood up and turned my whole chair around to view the dance floor. The chair separated clumsily from our closely packed table. Phyllis simply swung to the side of her seat, turning toward me. When she crossed her legs the slub of her black stocking rasped against my thigh, then rested there. Gwyn and Brandon led off, whirring giddily onto the wood-tiled platform just as the strains of Moonlight Serenade broke loose from long, ascending chords strung out by the orchestra as the build-up to these opening bars. Gwyn's head was thrown back, her mouth curled into an electric grin as Brandon whisked her vigorously atop the floor, smiling himself as he seemed to carry her. They blurred together, showing white black, white black, white black as he stepped her around. Her gown, his tuxedo, her gown—creamy elegance bestudded with beadwork that quite possibly some Honduran peasant lady had strung together while chomping a cigar. Did beads come from Honduras, I wondered. Her gown, his tuxedo—crisply draped and marshal, smoky black, he clutching her tightly around the waist. Spinning. Her gown, his tuxedo, her gown, his tuxedo, white, black, white, black. I tried to count up the number of times I had emptied my wine glass.

The music filled every space in the room that wasn't filled already with person or table or chair or wedding cake or chandelier. The sound seemed too much to hold. The best man led Anne onto the floor. He moved with the same easy confidence as Brandon. She seemed careful and cautious, wanting to watch where she was going as he whirred her around. Phyllis leaned close to my ear. "She's so beautiful," she whispered to me.

The others came out, ushers and bridesmaids paired as turning bodies that weaved together in a shifting mass, a cloud reshaping itself in distant wind. I closed my eyes. The trace of Phyllis's perfume lingered faintly around my head. I inhaled long, purposeful breaths. Did I smell it still, I wondered, or did my mind just hold the memory of it? If I could stay like this and never move again, I thought, my eyes still gently closed, it would remain with me, this spiced aroma set against the humid musk of her body. The orchestra swung on, saturating the large hall ever more densely with sound.

Her fingers closed invitingly around my wrist. "Come dance with me," said Phyllis. She spoke softly yet loudly above the assertion of the music. I looked back of me, left and right, at the others at the table. All of them watched us. Only Stephanie was smiling, a big, broad, loaded-with-life grin.

"Alex has to dance with his mother," Phyllis urged me. "I can't wait another second. Come dance with me."

By now the floor had filled with other couples. Still more were streaming up there, cutting through the sound-soaked air in long, broken files that snaked among the tables. Phyllis pulled me by my wrist toward them. At the edge of the dance floor she threw both arms around my neck, crossing them like scissors as I stepped instinctively to pack my body against hers. She arched supplely in response as I pressed her backward into the close pack of anonymous bodies, all of them moving like gusts to the music. It felt dark and intimate within the crowd. Phyllis pressed her lips in close to my ear and said, "This feels so good."

But then we stepped within sight of Anne. She was dancing with the best man still, though even he had lost his deft gaiety and seemed to be plodding outside of the music. Anne looked lifeless. Phyllis saw them too but I don't think she noticed their manner. She tugged me beside her as she stepped up to them, her whole face alight with a radiant grin.

"Look who I brought you," she said to Anne, who tried feebly to smile. "He's cutting in," she told the best man, laughing loudly above the persistence of the music. Then the two of them whirred off together, he regaining much of his bounce in a spontaneous shudder of liberation.

We locked arms but Anne wouldn't step close to me. She danced with her head down. I thought she was going to cry.

"I'm real sorry I can't dance as well as she can," she said.

"You dance just fine."

"Why did you have to bring him?"

"I tried to get rid of him. I brought him to my parents but my father had a breakdown. That's why I missed the wedding too. I'm really sorry."

She looked up at me, belief straining her face.

"What happened," she asked.

"I'm not exactly sure," I said, "because I wasn't there when it started. I can't get a straight story from dad, either. My mother cut her hand a little and I think that set him off. When I pulled up in the car he was already out of control. It was the worse I've ever seen anybody. I guess I should have seen it coming."

"Why?"

"Because he's been so depressed lately. I just never expected him to turn so agitated."

"What did he do?"

Her steps loosened gradually. We moved slowly, out of time with the music. We seemed separate from the crowd that way, isolated and alone, as if our miscadence distanced us from all the other dancers huddled in so closely around us, so we could talk more privately.

"By the time I got there he had busted all the windows out of the house," I explained. "He was throwing everything outside. Clothes. Dishes. Everything. He'd taken all the doors off, too. He said he wanted the weather and the birds to come in and destroy the place. I had to hold him down for a couple of minutes to get him to settle down."

Anne loosened more, her body acquiring a soft sway from my monotonous steps.

"I wanted to just drop the kid off with them and then go home and get ready. I would have had plenty of time. But I couldn't leave the place like that. I had to cover all the windows and get everything back inside. I had to make sure my father was all right, too."

"Is he okay," asked Anne.

"I think so. I think he's back to being just depressed again. But I don't know. By the time I finished everything I had to rush just to make it here. I didn't want to miss the reception too. Otherwise I would have found someplace else to take the kid."

"Just don't let him come near me," she said.

"I won't."

"I feel just terrible."

"So do I."

"I don't ever want him in our house again."

"I'll take him home right from here. I don't care if his mother is away or not. I don't care if the neighbors turn him in and the cops come and throw him in a foster home. There's nothing I can do about it."

The band sidled into its next song, dropping down the tempo. Anne and I were in rhythm now. We let the other dancers re-enter at our speed. We moved some paces silently. The music seemed less consuming. Everything moved so much slower now. In the calm that wrapped over me I worked my mind into resolutions: I would get rid of Trevor. I would apologize in earnest to Anne. I would do better by my parents, do something more than I'd been doing to help them along. What? It didn't matter. I felt like I already had things well in hand, and I rested, for a time, within the satisfaction of those thoughts and the swaying music.

But Gwyn appeared beside us in a happy agitation. She wanted Anne's help in making an adjustment to her gown. They needed to troop to the ladies' room together. Right away. It was the traditional routine: bride and attendant adjusting the gown after an early romp of dancing. I didn't see why one of the other bridesmaids couldn't help her, but Anne went away dutifully, though still not moving nearly as energetically as her sister.

I felt conspicuous again as I wended my way off the floor, weaving alone among the dancers, to find a place to finish out the evening. I would have preferred to finish it alone, but where can you hide at a wedding? I went back to my dinner table, the only place I could think to go.

Most of them were still there. It seemed a lot darker. Of course, Phyllis was gone, but I think the lights were down too. I

nodded the perfunctory hello again to everyone, who nodded back, or made some other such perfunctory gesture. Rita and Anita, Grace and all my six or eight in-laws here sat with their chairs turned facing the dance floor, magnets aligned to a pole, conversing privately among themselves. Some of their children, who had been seated with all the other kids in the back during dinner, had now joined the adults. Grace held her youngest on her lap. Another child, looking bored, leaned heavily against her side. After I settled into my abandoned seat I realized that the chair was turned around from the dancers and facing them all head on. They sat squared off against me like grand inquisitors. An illusion, I'm sure.

"Where did Stephanie go," I asked, mostly addressing her father, Anita's husband. If this was a pose for a family photo, he would have been the patriarch, being the oldest. Everyone seemed to be ignoring him, too, which can be another sure sign of patriarchy.

"She's up there dancing," he replied.

"Good for her," I said.

Anita turned away.

"How was your dance with Phyllis," Rita sniped. "Does she dance as well as she does everything else?"

"She dances very well."

"I bet."

"Did you see her roots," asked Anita. "While you were gone we decided she's a Clairol blonde."

"I don't think so. Her roots looked pretty real to me."

"Are you kidding. A blonde like that is one in a million."

"Well, maybe she's that one."

"We can ask Stephie when she gets back," said her father, the patriarch, putting an end to the squabble. "She got a closer look than any of us." Actually, I had gotten the closest look, but I accepted his mediation.

"Did you make up with Anne yet," Rita asked me.

"We were just dancing. Didn't you see us?"

"That's nice," she answered, meaning it, I think. "Does she feel better now?"

"A little bit. She's pretty worn out. It's been a tough day for her. It's been tough on both of us. In fact, I think I'm going to get out of here pretty soon."

Roger returned to the table, two hands clasped tenuously around the bundle of drinks he'd just fetched from the bar. Seeing me here he grinned broadly. "Hey, have you seen your son lately," he asked me.

"I've barely seen him since we got here," I said. "Why? What's he doing?"

"He's cleaning up the place. He's going around to all the empty tables and finishing the drinks people left."

I shot up immediately, making for the table by the bar in the back, the table where he had eaten dinner with the down-dressed rich kids, the table where I had assumed, foolishly, he would remain inconspicuously throughout the evening. As I skirted the dance floor I crossed Anne, who threw me an icy look that could only mean that I was too late. She had seen him already. I veered off and followed her, walking fast to catch up because she was moving so fast. She stopped at the far side of the hall, fully across from the orchestra and its dancers, in an unused edge of the room where the lights were turned off and where some extra tables were stowed. The music barely reached here. It sounded distant. When she sensed me just a step behind her she turned around and raged.

"How could you bring him here?"

"I had to," I pleaded. "I didn't have any choice. I already explained all that."

"You should have known he would do something like this."

"Like what?"

"He's drunk."

"I'm going to get him out of here right away. That's where I was going just now. To take him away."

"It doesn't matter now. Everybody has already seen him."

"No they haven't. It's not too late."

Then Trevor arrived, coming up behind me and provoking a grimace of despair from Anne that told me he was here before I even saw him.

"Where'd you go," he said to me, slurring the words boozily. "I been lookin' for you all over the place."

"Come on," I told him. "I'm taking you home."

"Hey, Mrs. Hectorman," he said, "you know, you're really aw right."

"Let's go." I pulled his arm.

"No, no, I really mean dat." He planted his feet. "I know I never said nothin' like this before. But I really mean it. This here . . . I never been to a wedding before."

"Let's go."

"I never been to anything like this in my whole life before. I can see now . . . you know. Like, it lets me see what yer really like. Not just my teacher anymore."

"I said come on."

"Yer really a' right. From now on I'm gonna work really hard in yer class. Yewl see. From now on I'm gonna be yer star pupil. I'm gonna git a A."

Anne snapped. She reared up and swarmed down on him. "You've already ruined my class. And now you've ruined my sister's wedding."

He backed off a step, then stopped to regather himself, the adjustment working slowly, visibly, the booze having slowed even the swing of his feelings, his sensations murking through syrup. He blinked his eyes and wagged his head around, as though he had to move it to make his thoughts move inside.

"You doan have to be so hyper," he mouthed slowly. "I aw'ready said I was sorry n' ev'thing."

"You're not sorry. You're drunk. You're disgusting. What gives you the right to do this to me? I was supposed to be helping you. That class could have been the best thing that ever happened to you. But you ruined it. You ruined it for yourself and for everyone else, too."

"I din't ruin it. It just i'n't very good."

I took a firmer grip on his arm and tugged hard. He fell. I kept hold to keep him from going down too violently. He stayed there, splayed on the floor, his legs stuck out flaccidly, his head roving slowly around as he tried to comprehend the sudden change in the room's perspective. He didn't yet realize he was on the floor. Anne bent over him. "I want you out of my class," she hissed. She looked up at me. "I want him out of my class."

Working like a forklift I scooped him through the armpits and pried him off the floor. He couldn't quite pull his feet under him. I dragged him away anyway, his heels skidding the floor.

"It's no' my fault," he shouted to Anne. "T'e other kids, dey just don' like it."

I got him fully back on his feet before we reached the crowd-filled reception area. I held him by the back of his pants—my pants—to try to keep him from weaving too much. I should have made straight for the door. Instead I suffered an impulse to say a proper farewell to the bridal couple, to hug them and wish them well on their journey and all. Blind protocol again. As if things wouldn't be so bad if only I exited according to the laws of etiquette. Maybe I expected Anne to see it. I plopped Trevor into a chair at an empty table on the outer fringes of the seating area.

"Don't you dare move," I told him. "I'm coming right back and we're getting out of here." I pointed a sharp finger at him, as if that would hold him in my absence. His head ratcheted slowly from side to side as he tried to take in the scene again. He wasn't comprehending. Or, if he was, he comprehended according to the new-found sensations of a first drunk, which is what makes a person drink again. His thoughts pushed pleasantly through putty. I rushed away, to get back all the sooner.

I wanted to find Brandon and Gwyn quickly. The bar seemed the center of action. I went directly there. A hand reached out and pulled me into a group as I passed. It was Phyllis.

"There you are," she said. "I've been looking all over for you. I wanted to introduce you to Alex, only—this is so embarrassing—I can't remember your name."

"I'm Dan," I said hastily. "I'm looking for Gwyn and . . ."

"Alex," she said, pulling me deeper within the group. "Alex, this is who I was telling you about." He turned from another conversation.

"Oh, hello, Danny," he said, shaking my hand.

"You already know him," Phyllis asked, disappointed.

"Sure. We met last night."

"He's Anne's husband," she said.

"I know."

"He's a marvelous dancer."

"You look like you're having a good time," he said to me.

"Actually, I'm on my way out."

"Really?"

"You can't leave so soon," Phyllis protested.

"I have to take someone home."

"Then you can come back," she said hopefully.

"Maybe."

"You'd better tell her you'll come back or she'll never let you leave."

"Okay. I'll come back."

"No you won't. You're just saying that."

"Do you know where Gwyn and Brandon are?"

"I'll probably never get to see you again."

"Yes you will," I said. "Alex and I are like brothers-in-law now." I peered over her head, panning for the white smear of a wedding dress among the many people. Alex turned back into his earlier conversation, abandoning us.

"I don't care about Alex," Phyllis said. "He's being a big bore today. Dance with me now, for old time's sake, before you leave."

"I really have to leave now."

She tugged me, extracting me toward the music.

"Will you help me find Gwyn and Brandon? I just wanted to say good-bye."

"After we dance."

"I've really gotta get out of here."

"After we dance."

She flung both arms around my neck and I placed my hands on her hips, keeping back half a step and trying so damn desperately to resist the urge to tuck into her. I failed. She stepped in to meet me, sending my two hands sliding around her back, feeling the brush of her bare skin lightly perspiring.

Trying hard to focus my eyes I looked over her head but saw no sign of the newlyweds. Her color was natural. We turned and turned and turned. The music seemed louder than before. A woman had come out to sing with the orchestra. Someone to Watch Over Me. We turned and turned. I slid up a hand and let it rest, lightly cupped, atop the deft extrusion of a scapula. Phyllis shifted nearer. We turned. I couldn't see them anywhere.

When the song ended we coasted slowly to a stop, an iron wheel winding down its momentum. Phyllis stepped back from me and clapped slowly and softly, her fingers arched back so that only her palms touched.

"Wasn't that wonderful," she said. "Don't you just love to dance?" Then her face lit at the sight of something beyond me. She grabbed my wrist again. "There's Brandon and Gwyn," she said. "I think they're going to go cut the cake now. Let's go see 'em." She brought me along with my arm like a leash.

But I didn't make it. The thick-set girl in the short leather skirt angled across the floor to intercept me. Her expression of urgency stopped me cold. My wrist pulled free from the grasp of Phyllis, who scampered away without even stopping to see that we had separated.

"Your son is passed out in the ladies' room," the girl said to me.

"He's not my son." But I followed her dutifully as she steamed back toward the bathroom.

Stephanie was there with him, kneeling beside him with the grave look of a medic ministering to a casualty on a battlefield. But he was only dead drunk. A woman walking out glared at me with disgust as she stepped around us.

"He came in here and threw up in the toilet," the big girl said. "We tried to get him out but he passed out right here. We can't move him."

A stall door slammed. A woman strode toward us. Anne. She had been crying. She focused on me an expression distilled from disdain and remorse and loathing and fear. The face a witness wears in sight of a killing. She blasted past us and banged out the door.

"It's not his fault," said Stephanie. "I was at their table for a while. After I was dancing. The others put him up to it. They dared him. They got him to do it because they didn't have enough guts to do it themselves. They took advantage of him. I think they're jealous of him."

"Right. Of course," said the girl in black. "Look at how much he has for us to be jealous over."

Stephanie glared up at her. "At least he's genuine," she said.

"Genuine? And what are we? Holograms?"

"You're Bob Dylans. He's James Dean."

"Huh? James Dean was an actor, too, you know."

"Help me get him out of here," I said to Stephanie.

"Where are you going to take him," she asked.

"To my car."

"You're not just going to leave him out there, are you? I mean, I don't think it's safe to leave him alone when he's like this."

"I'm going to drive him home. Now, come on. Let's just get him out of here."

I hefted him up from under his arms like before, but this time his body was wholly limp and unresponsive. He remained unconscious. It was like lifting stones in a sack.

"Jesus," I complained. "How much did he drink?"

"He drank a lot," said the big girl. "He drank every drink he could steal when people weren't looking."

"Is he okay," Stephanie asked.

"He's fine. In the morning he'll be perfectly fine, unless I kill him before that."

"Are you sure?"

"Trust me."

I held him up on one side, but I was wavering under the dead-weight, and Stephanie was having a hard time maneuvering in to help support him.

"Here. Let me try," said the other girl. She ducked under his arm and held it fast across her shoulders. She wrapped her other arm around his waist and locked in competently. With Stephanie holding open the bathroom door we dragged him out together, scurrying quickly around the bar toward a hidden side exit that the girl pointed out to me. In the car I tried to wake him, but he was gone completely. I didn't linger long to wonder how I could get him into his apartment—how I could carry him inside the building and where I would find a key and what the neighbors would think when they saw us. In the end I just drove him back to my house. I knew Anne wouldn't be coming home tonight anyway.

CHAPTER NINE

I left him in the car to sleep it off. I rolled open the sedan's windows and I cracked open a cobweb-encased sash in the back wall of the garage, worrying vaguely about chemical smells. I remember plodding upstairs to my lonely bedroom, but I must have dropped off very soundly after that because it was late morning by the time I awoke. I cursed myself for forgetting to set the alarm, because I had wanted to get up to get Trevor out of here early, before Anne arrived. I had no idea what time she might come home, though I could easily guess that it wouldn't be early. But just the same I wanted him long gone, with no traces left. Trevor was awake and sitting up in the car when I got to the garage. He realized I would be shuttling him home. He was waiting for me.

Later that same day—in fact, it was late that evening—Rita arrived to pick up some clothing for Anne. When I first heard her car I thought she was my wife, come home at last, at about the same time she had returned one week ago, after her slumber-party cum bridal-shower weekend away. Tomorrow started the work week, after all, and the pull of professional obligation was forcing her back to her house, back to me, back, eventually, to a make up and reconciliation. Or so I thought. When the doorbell rang my spirits sagged. I knew it couldn't be Anne. Rita walked past me into the house before she announced that Anne wasn't coming home, and that she had come to collect some clothes for her to wear to work in the morning.

"This is ridiculous," I said to her. "Where is she going to sleep?"

"She's staying at my house tonight. But that's just for one night. Tomorrow she's moving in to Gwyn's, because they're away for a month on their honeymoon now."

"A month!"

"She doesn't really know if she'll stay there that long. She doesn't really know what she'll do. That's the thing: she needs some time to sort everything out."

"Everything? What do you mean by everything?"

"You know: everything that's happened between you two."

"But nothing's happened. We had a fight. That's all. Yesterday was a bad day. Maybe we've had a bad couple of weeks. But isn't this kind of extreme?"

"I know," said Rita. "I don't know what to tell you. She has to tell you all this herself but she just couldn't bring herself to come here tonight. That's why I got here so late. She kept telling herself she was coming but she kept putting it off and it got later and later until we just couldn't wait any longer. So I came. She needs some things from her bedroom."

"It's our bedroom. And what am I supposed to do in the meantime? We need to work this out."

"I think that's the problem," Rita volunteered. "I think she's afraid you'll work it out and then she'll be trapped again."

"Trapped? That's a hell of a way to put it. What do you mean by trapped?"

"I don't know what it means. That's what Anne said. I'm just repeating it to you. You have to ask her what it means. But if you ask me, I think she's afraid."

"Afraid? Afraid of what?"

"Afraid that she's kind of, you know, running out of time. She said there's just nothing happening in her life. She doesn't feel like she's going anywhere."

"Not going anywhere? Well, where does she want to go?"

"She doesn't know. That's the problem. There's no direction. No progress. She keeps saying that she just feels like she's running out of time. Like she's not getting anywhere. She had put so much hope in her new class this year. She thought it was the start of something . . . you know, something important. But now she says that it's all falling apart too, so she feels like she's back to nowhere."

"That's not her fault. It's falling apart because now the big thinkers at the school are losing interest in it, because now there's other grant money to get. I told her that would happen. That's how it always goes with these things: they come and they go. I warned her about that. Now a newer fad is taking up all their time. I don't even know what it's called this year—something they're calling parent partnerships, I think. They've already forgotten about Anne's B-section. B-section is going to just fade away now. I warned her about that."

"Whatever."

"This is just too damn sudden."

"I don't know. I think I saw it coming a while ago."

"Can I come over and talk to her?"

"No. She doesn't want that."

Rita came back the next evening to retrieve a larger cache of clothing. She all but emptied Anne's closet and drawers of the warm-weather stuff, leaving behind only the woolens and thermal wear that lingered from the cold season that now seemed so distant, the things that wouldn't be needed again until the next inevitable arctic blast that still waited so far in the future.

"You don't have to take her bathing suit, too," I protested, watching from behind her as Rita scraped to the bottom of Anne's bottom drawer, pushing the last few pieces of clothing into shopping bags that now bulged.

"I know," she said. "But I told her I'd just get everything."

"But she's not going to need her bathing suit."

"You never know."

Anne's few heavy coats and sweaters and turtlenecks and silk longjohns that remained in the room made the place more desolate than it would have seemed if it was just plain empty. Ancient ruins in a desert, isolated, hinting at unsustained presence.

But as bleak as the house now seemed, I stayed on hopefully. This was my home, after all. Or, more encouragingly, it was our home. I remained in a state of keen anticipation those few days, expecting that every moment would be the moment in which my wife would return. I would drive home from work and race into the driveway and crane impatiently, as the garage door rolled upward, to see if her car was inside. At odd times throughout each evening I stretched up from my chair in the living room to look out to the end of the driveway, on the off chance that this would be the instant Anne's car would swing in off the street. We would have it out. I'd take the drubbing I deserved for the hash I had made of the wedding. Then we would make up, and our life together would resume. That was my earnest expectation, because continuity is every person's constant expectation, with each successive moment arriving with its own presumption of invincibility, with the certain assumption that we'll stumble into a next moment that's pretty much the same as the one just past. Yet changes come, unanticipated, sculpting contours in time.

The third evening Rita arrived that week she came only to deliver the news: tomorrow Anne was going to see a lawyer. "She wants me to tell you that she would have come to tell you that herself, but she knew you'd only try to change her mind. She doesn't want that. She says she finally made up her mind that this is what she wants to do and she doesn't want you to talk her out of it. But she said that she owes you the courtesy of telling you first, before she goes and does it. That's why I came."

"A lawyer?"

"She wants the separation to be legal and binding and all of that. She says that's the only way she can pick things up and start moving again. She says she can't start something else until this is finished."

"But it isn't finished."

"Anne thinks it is."

"But you said separation. She only wants a separation and not a divorce, right?"

"Well, that's what she says right now."

"Don't let her go see a lawyer," I pleaded. "It'll be over for sure. That'll make it all so final."

"But she wants it to be final. I just told you that."

"You don't know what I mean. With a lawyer it isn't just the two of us anymore. It's us and the system. If it's only us then there's some hope. But if it's us and the system, then there's all the damn rules and procedures and regulations and requirements and everything. Once you get into the system you can't work it out. You're locked in to their way. You're trapped. You're doomed."

"She warned me you'd be like this. That's why she didn't want to come herself."

"That I would get like what? I'm not like anything. I just don't want everything to get all messed up."

"Everything already is all messed up."

I had no response for that.

"That's all I wanted to tell you," Rita said. "I'd better go now."

"Wait. Not yet. I need you to tell her something for me."

"Well? What is it?"

"Tell her I'll do anything she wants if she'll just hold off on the lawyer."

"But she wants a separation."

"Then I'll give her that."

"How?"

"I'll move out. She can have the house. All to herself. For as long as she wants."

"What difference will that make?"

"She'll be more comfortable here. She'll sleep better. Things like that. You know. All her things are here and everything, and she knows where everything is. The kitchen and everything. It'll be a lot better than staying with someone else. She won't feel like she's in the way."

"But you'd be coming around all the time."

"No I won't. Not if she doesn't want me to."

"Then where will you live?"

"I'll get an apartment. That way she'll know I'm serious."

"Why don't you want her to see a lawyer so badly?"

"I've seen what they can do."

"Anne told me you'd get like this."

"I just don't want any lawyers involved."

"They'll have to get involved sooner or later."

"Then let it be later. Tell Anne I'll move out tonight if she wants me to. I won't bother her at all. I won't even call her to tell her I'm gone. She can call me when she's ready to talk. How more separated can you get?"

"I'll tell her," said Rita, "but I don't think she'll go for it."

About an hour later Rita telephoned to tell me that I would have to be out of the house by Sunday morning for Anne to accept my offer. She told me to take everything I might need, not just clothes and a toothbrush but any tools and books and papers and supplies and anything—but only my things—that I might conceivably try to sneak back to retrieve later on. There would be no sneaking back, she assured me.

But what about pots and pans and plates and glasses and spoons, I wondered. I could easily enough take half the plates and half the glasses, but there was only one big soup pot between us, and one set of mixing bowls and only one everyday frying pan. Who should get the extra soap we kept in the bathroom cabinet under the sink for when the bar in the shower shrank down? Who should take the tube of toothpaste we'd already opened? What about the ketchup in the fridge? The loose change in the cup on the dresser? The matchbooks stuffed into the jar way in the back of the cupboard? What about the flashlight? The alarm clock? The little TV on the stand in the bedroom?

It was all corporate property, of course, and any lawyer

would tell me it belonged with the house. I had already ceded the house to Anne. I left the stuff without a quibble. I left a lot more, too. Like my life insurance policy, which named Anne as its beneficiary anyway. I left some old books saved from college in a box in the little crawl space upstairs. I left the suits and overcoats that had grown gradually too tight, the one Trevor had worn, and the others still hanging in plastic bags in the spare closet because I harbored the vain hope that I could eventually trim pounds enough to squeeze myself into them again. I left my old baseball glove. I hadn't picked it up in years anyway, and I was all out of room in the boxes I had scrounged from the grocer. I crammed the bulging crates into my car and even tied a few precariously to the roof to cart them away to my parents house. My agreement with Anne required me to find an apartment, to prove that I was willing to leave her alone and, even, to abandon all hope of ever bothering her again. But I would need at least a little time to find a rental place. I'd wait till the end of the month, which was the first I'd be able to pick up a lease anyway.

Besides, it turned out that despite our agreement Anne sicced a lawyer on me anyway. She had me served with papers at my office just a few days after I moved into my old bedroom in the old house I'd dozed in so comfortably as a boy. The process came off with its characteristically cold and oily efficiency, the young man neatly dressed in a sport shirt buttoned around his bulging neck, asking for me politely by name from Tweed and then politely addressing me as "sir," but edging the word, probably to call still more attention to the plain-as-day fact that the girth of his arms were double mine. The paperwork said I was being sued for legal separation from marriage, and went on, presumably, to explain all the details in inhumanly dense language that hid behind its cold precision. I didn't read it all, and I wanted to shred it and crumple it and stomp on it and burn it. But the husky young man had served it publicly in my office, in full view of Tweed and a few others, a move calculated to produce witnesses, should I later deny ever receiving it—though I toyed with the idea anyway.

Taking the advice of a couple of my unconcerned associates, I took a lawyer of my own. The unwritten rules of the game pretty much stipulate that whenever you retain an attorney you relinquish all authority to him, the way you let a surgeon decide if it's a good idea to cut out your heart and stitch in a replacement from a dead person. After the attorneys took their retainers, Anne and I became only marginal characters in our own undoing. All the action instead involved the two lawyers—plus their bevies of masked and hidden clerks and secretaries. The problem was, each of the attorneys also had dozens of other clients, all of them certainly much different than us, who were involved in actions of their own that were much different than ours, though each was individually complicated in its own right. And with so many of us to shepherd, the attorneys didn't really have the time, talent or raw creative energy to give any one of our actions the personal attention it required. So that no matter how important our individual issues seemed to us, to our separate attorneys they were just additional professional obligations that they just didn't have time to get to right away, with so many other professional obligations pressing so urgently. Therefore they handled the teetering disposition of my marriage by bouncing letters back and forth between the two of them, then dutifully sending mere photocopies of the letters, separately, to Anne and me. The process created at least the illusion that things were moving forward, because it provided the two lawyers with new documents to periodically send to their clients, presumably to appease us. But the letters were so damn dense and, at the same time, so damn trite that they couldn't capture my interest. I could never find any words about my marriage in them. After a while I stopped reading them altogether. It seemed better to simply stick with my first instinct to leave all the joint property with the house. I retreated with only the clothes on my back, and whatever else I held in the bulging boxes stashed at my mother and father's house.

CHAPTER TEN

S ometimes in college, and even for a while after that, I occasionally woke peacefully in the serene, still morning hours before light imagining dreamily that I was in my childhood bed in my childhood bedroom upstairs in my parents' house. It was a comfortable hallucination, or maybe just a dream, immersing me deeply once again within all the cuddlesome security of boyhood, with its unwavering assumption of immortality, when joy and happiness and contentment arrived at the end of each fulfillment of every biological impulse, like eating, touching warmth, hearing the familial voice of my parents. But always the hallucination gradually faded. My eyes slowly focused on peculiar details within the room around me, making me realize that I wasn't in my old bedroom at all, making me disoriented and anxious then because I couldn't remember where I was sleeping. Why wasn't I in bed in my room, I worried, until my sense of present circumstances gradually returned to me as my mind rose nearer to wakefulness. With weary disappointment I realized that I was in my dormitory room, or in the cube-shaped little garret room I rented down on Ninth Street, or in some other late-made bed. Finally fully awake, I laid alone with the chill reality, missing the worn old walls that had so comfortably contained the first eighteen years of my life.

Yet deep into my first night back in the same homesteading bedroom I had missed for so long, deep into my first night of official exile from the marriage bed I had shared with Anne, I awoke in the sudden quiet and didn't recognize the place. My head felt dozy still and befuddled, and I looked out into the grainy dark trying to latch my eyes onto the hull of some familiar object: the dresser over by the window, or maybe the little TV on the stand. But the faint outlines that returned to me were foreign and unfamiliar. I looked harder, waking more quickly now as a dim panic stirred upward through my confusion. I wasn't at home. I wasn't in my bed. Where could I be?

When I turned for Anne but found myself alone in the cramped bed it came to me. I was upstairs in my old bedroom in my parents' house. She wasn't here.

I tried hard to remember what it felt like sleeping with her beside me in bed. Or rather, I tried to recreate the sense of it. To feel the faint pull of her gravity, light bodies in space. To breath the air of her quiet exhale. But it had been so long since I had paid any attention to the commonplace subtleties of the woman. It's how all marriages end. The closest I came to bringing her back that night was the resurrection of the memory of how every morning during our early marriage I wrapped my arm atop my wife, and sometimes a leg as well as we laid together through the indistinct moments before rising, after quieting the clock's urgent alarm, lazy in comfort, before the call of morning duties wedged us apart. We were newly married still. It had become our habit for maybe a month or two. Maybe three. Maybe six. I couldn't remember exactly when the ritual had ended. I couldn't think of any reason why it had ended. Still, the fact was unassailable now : sometime ago Anne and I had stopped embracing in the morning and sometime later we slept alone.

CHAPTER ELEVEN

I dozed. Later I awoke again through another mist of confusion and displacement. I felt lost again in the unfamiliar bed. But I felt something more as well: someone was here. I sensed the presence before I even opened my eyes. Staring through the dimness I latched narrowly onto the figure of my father, swaddled in baggy pajamas over by the door, hesitant and indecisive, not wholly in the room and not wholly outside of it either. He looked stooped and bent and worn. He looked dispossessed. A stray. Homeless and wandering. I stared at the image. I wondered if it was really him. Maybe I was dreaming. Or maybe this was his wan spirit. The room was dark still but brightening with the approach of morning. I didn't know if he could see that my eyes were open and watching him.

"What time is it?" I said at last, partly to see if he would answer, to test if the presence in the door was really him.

"She's at it again," he said, seizing the opening, approaching my bed quickly now, as if he was being pushed all the sudden from behind.

"She's at what?"

"Your mother. She's acting up again. She does this all the time now. I never get any sleep any more. I can't take this."

"What's wrong?"

"She kept me up all night. I never even dozed off. I have to watch her all the time. I can't take any more of this."

"How long have you been standing there?"

"I don't know. Not long. What difference does it make?"

"How long have you been awake?"

"I've been awake all night. I just told you that. I can't sleep with you staying here."

"Why not?"

"Because of your mother. It upsets her too much. She kept me awake all night."

The room was brighter now from dawn's rising. I could see him clearly. He looked unsubstantial, a frame of sagging wire kinked beneath crumpled pajamas, his head a ball just stuck on top.

"I didn't sleep too well either," I said.

"That's different. You—you got your own problems. But this here has been going on for a long time. I can't put up with it anymore."

"What is she doing?"

"What is she doing! She's doing what she always does. I have to watch her every minute. And then I get so worked up that I can't get to sleep."

"I didn't hear anything last night. I was awake most of the night myself and I never heard a sound."

"Ouph," he groaned, exasperated, physically unable to

speak, struggling now simply to suck in and force out air alone, absent the utterances. He shuddered and trembled and gulped in more air. "She fell asleep after a while," he said at last. "It was earlier that she was acting up. Just after you got here. She . . . she . . . ouph."

I waited. He might have been pausing for breath or pausing from confusion. "What did she do," I asked him at last.

"She was all worked up about your being here. About you leaving your wife. You don't belong here."

"I know I don't. But Anne threw me out. I don't have anyplace else to go right now. It's only temporary. I'll only be here for a little while. Maybe just a few days."

"You can't stay here," he said. "I would have told you that last night when you got here but I couldn't get a moment away from Elizabeth. She wanted to come up here and make up the bed for you and she was worried that the room wasn't cleaned. All she does now is go around wanting to do things. I went out to do some work in the yard and when I came in I found her in the bathroom with a bucket of water. She didn't even remember what she wanted to do with it. She just stands there with it. Then she gets all worked up when I try to get her to sit down. Yesterday she pushed me out of her way and I almost fell down."

"It's not personal," I told him. "She doesn't mean it. You already know all that. It's her condition. The Alzheimer's. She gets frightened because she's so confused."

"That's easy for you to say. Your wife never pushed you over like that."

"My wife just threw me out."

"You can't stay here," he repeated. "Things are screwed up enough around here already. I can't take it the way things are now. I don't know how much more of this I can stand."

"It's only temporary," I assured him. "Until I find another place. Until I figure out exactly what's going to happen."

"You should be at home with your wife."

"I can use the time I'm here to help you get things fixed up a little."

He looked around the room, dumbfounded and confused, as if this new idea of mine needed more time to penetrate his monothinking. His gaze lingered on the busted-out window taped over with a plastic sheet by Trevor a week before.

"There's all these windows to fix," I told him. "We have to get them replaced before the mosquitoes start coming in."

"I can't keep up with anything anymore," he said.

"I can help you while I'm here."

"I don't think I can take much more of this."

"You have to relax. It'll be okay. Don't take everything she does so personally. She doesn't seem that unmanageable to me."

"Of course she doesn't to you. You're not around here all the time. You don't see how she behaves when you're not around. She has good days and bad days sometimes. You don't see her on the bad days. Some days she does just fine but other times she's like a whole different person. It's just too much for me. I can't keep up with it anymore."

"What time is it," I asked. "I have to get ready for work soon. I looked for a clock. I used to keep a small one here on the nightstand by the bed, but things had changed. This wasn't my room anymore. I tried to remember where I had placed my wristwatch when I had climbed into bed so late last night. The room was very jumbled with the bags and boxes I had carried in from the car in the dark. I remembered that the light on the ceiling overhead didn't work. I'd discovered that last night. I wondered where my parents kept the spare light bulbs now. I wondered how I could get ready from all of these things piled in boxes all around me now. What would I find to wear? Where were my razor and toothbrush?

"Do you know what time it is," I asked my father more directly.

He stood silently for a moment, as if he was alone, or as if he just hadn't heard the question. At last he responded, "it must be getting close to morning."

"I have to get up and get dressed," I announced. "We can talk about this when I get back this afternoon. I think everything will be all right if you can just settle down and relax a little. I can help you with things now."

"How can I relax? Every time I turn around she's up to something different. I can't find time to do the things I have to do around here, and with Elizabeth, she's always making more. I can't keep up with it anymore."

"Everything will be fine," I told him. "Like I said, now that I'm here I can help you. We'll get everything fixed up and straightened out again."

"This place is such a mess," he moaned. "Just look at it. The whole house is falling apart. I just can't keep up with it anymore."

But I only wanted a roof over my head and four concealing walls, and some time and some quiet to salve my gashes. But where could I find them now? I hadn't counted on Peter's craziness. I had never expected him to welcome me, but I had hoped that at least he would leave me alone. Now where was I going to go?

CHAPTER TWELVE

I went to work. Naturally I arrived there late, staying inside my well-worn pattern. But this morning, instead of my usual discontent, I felt almost relieved to be there. Almost. If only I didn't have to see any appointments.

Tweed had arrived well before me, uncharacteristic for her. Carmelita was thoroughly vanquished. Vivian Tweed was back at all her strength, strutting in full swagger, bursting into my office to tell me about her husband's return. Alfred had come home on Saturday, begging her to take him back. That was the same day I had started loading up boxes with my salvaged possessions to carry out of my own home with Anne. My former home with Anne. Still, I told Tweed I was happy for her.

And oh, Tweed reminded me as she left my office, I needed to get ready for my first appointment, with Joan Petrochelli. I cringed.

Joan Petrochelli and her husband, Julian, were typical manipulators, parents who tortured school services to win any advantage for their child. I saw the type often. Anxious, covetous, insecure, but at the same time insistent and demanding, they wanted a trophy child, a badge, like a Mercedes in the driveway. The Petrochellis' current gambit was to have their child diagnosed with attention deficit hyperactivity disorder, or ADHD. It once was called simply hyperactivity, and for a while after that it was attention deficit disorder, or ADD. Psychologists, like professionals in so many fields, rename things often, because professionals in the field need new things to write about in journals read by professionals in the field. Little Warren Petrochelli was a child in grade three. But his parents were thinking ahead. If he was diagnosed with attention deficit hyperactivity disorder, the payoffs could follow him throughout his academic career. In high school, during the college-admission lottery – a far-off event that competitive, image-obsessed parents like the Petrochellis nonetheless schemed for early – children with ADHD received an unlimited time period to complete important tests like the Scholastic Aptitude Test, the SAT. Every other high-school kid, of course, sweated the SAT within rigidly enforced time periods. But the unlimited spans granted to ADHD kids were considered fair compensation for their inbred inability to concentrate. The Petrochellis already had run their Warren through the batteries of doctor visits and psychological evaluations necessary to get him the ADHD stamp. I was their final hoop to jump. With my signature, little Warren would be officially classified as subnormal, so that he could outperform his peers.

They expected this step to be merely procedural, a simple formality. Mrs. Petrochelli came alone. Her husband, she told me, was traveling on business. I thought that might make the meeting more tolerable. Her husband had dominated our prior sessions. Maybe Joan Petrochelli would be more docile with Julian absent.

Besides, Joan Petrochelli was stunningly shaped, with deep contours etched above undulant hips. If I had to deal with just one Petrochelli, Joan was the clear choice over Julian.

"You realize," I said to her, speaking slowly to sound thoughtful, "you realize that hyperactivity was, traditionally, thought to occur in only a small percentage of the total population?"

"I thought they didn't call it that anymore?"

"You mean 'hyperactivity'?"

"Now everybody calls it ADHD."

"I was just using the colloquial term."

"We just don't think our son should be penalized for having this condition that isn't his fault. We just want him to have what he's entitled to," she said.

"Of course you do," I replied. "We're all interested in the same thing, in doing what's right for Warren. What I'm supposed to do is make sure this is the right thing. You know: that we're not going so far with something that we'll end up hurting him instead of helping him."

"But everyone else says he has it. I don't see why you're being so difficult."

"I'm not being difficult. It's just my responsibility to go through this stuff. That's why they designed the system this way, with a lot of checks and balances and everything so we can be absolutely sure that we're doing the right thing when we finally do do something."

"But we know him better than anybody. We're his parents."

"Of course you do. It's just that, well, I'm starting to get signals that some parents are taking advantage of the ADHD diagnosis. I'm just trying to weed out any abuse before it really gets to be a problem."

"Well, who would want to abuse something like that?"

"You'd be surprised," I told her. "I'm seeing some parents try to use it to give their children an unfair advantage, because they get to take more time on tests and things like that if they're thought to have ADHD."

I thought she might blush at least a little from this. But Mrs. Petrochelli was unflinching.

"But so many of you have seen Warren already," she said. "First we had to bring him to his own pediatrician. Then to a specialist. We've been to everybody. I don't think everyone would say he had it if he didn't. Even his teacher says he has it."

"A lot of people make a lot of money evaluating kids, and you get more kids to evaluate when your tests come out the way the parents want them to. Besides, sometimes teachers like to see some kids drugged out on Ritalin." I wasn't supposed to say that.

"It doesn't drug them out," retorted Joan Petrochelli. "Everybody says it's completely safe. That's why so many people use it."

"I'm only trying to make a point," I said. "And no drug is completely safe. That's why you have to have a prescription to use it. That's why we have this approval process with all these checks and balances and everything."

"But I know all that," insisted Mrs. Petrochelli, whose salon-glossed hair began to look the duller to me.

"Okay. I'm sure you do. But like I said, we have to go through this, for Warren's sake. It's not just the drug. There's other things, too. We want to make sure he won't feel stigmatized, for instance."

"There's no stigma," she shot back at me. "Why would there be any stigma? It's like he's sick. Well, not sick. But he has a condition. That's it: a condition. He can't help it. Why would there be any stigma for that?"

"There shouldn't be. But you can't really control what other people think. Especially not school kids."

"But why would they think any less of him?"

"Because saying he has ADHD is saying he's, well, it's saying he's different from them. It's saying that he needs more time to do things that they might be able to do without a second thought. They might see that as being deficient."

"But he's not deficient."

"But they might see it that way."

"He's just as smart as everybody else."

"But with ADHD you're saying that he isn't the same."

"We're not saying that about his intelligence."

"But I'm talking about the way people might interpret it."

"Besides," she reasoned, "when he takes the Ritalin, he'll be the same as everybody else anyway, right?"

"I don't know. It's really impossible to say." Besides, there was a good chance he wouldn't even take the Ritalin, because other kids would urge him to squirrel away the pills and sell them in the school yard for cash to buy other things. Maybe other drugs. But I didn't go into that argument because by now I had abandoned all hope for Mrs. Petrochelli.

"Okay," I said, "the last thing I have to do is schedule one last visit with Warren."

"What for," she asked me.

"Just to make sure that he meets all the criteria."

"What criteria," she demanded. "Everybody already says he has ADHD."

"We just have to make sure."

"We already are sure."

"But there might be another way to handle it. It might not really be that big of a problem."

"What else could it be? Are you trying to say my son is normal?"

"Well, he just might be normal."

"He's not normal. How could he be? Everyone says he has attention desficit hyperact . . . he has disorder. He has attention desfi . . . attention defs. . . he has ADHD."

"Sometimes kids just act out."

"My Warren doesn't act out. Are you saying my Warren acts out? Are you saying my Warren is just a discipline problem?"

"No. I'm not saying that at all." There was no point in arguing, after all. Clearly little Warren was doomed. And if I went much farther to rescue him, I could be courting real trouble with his parents. Nothing riles ADHD parents more than hints of blame, guilt and retribution aimed at them.

"I just want to see him one last time. I need a little more time to put through all the paperwork anyway." Paperwork: the one unassailable excuse for any delay. "I'll get him in here as soon as I can."

"When?"

"Probably in a couple of days. Maybe by the end of the week. I'll have Mrs. Tweed set it up today."

"We've been waiting so long already."

"It won't be much longer," I assured her with grave honesty. "Keep in mind that what we're doing here is going to affect him for the rest of his life."

"I know."

"Okay."

I was quite anxious for her to go.

While she sat, unsatisfied still, I glanced hopefully at my appointment schedule, anticipating some open time. I drooped when I saw that William Lauxhaul was due to see me right after Petrochelli finished. Lauxhaul was involved in a parents dispute. He was ringleader of a warring faction within of the junior high school parents guild. Lauxhaul's group had been in charge of organizing the school's annual father/daughter breakfast hosted for eighth grade students each spring, one of several rites of passage upward to the high school. It should have been a routine affair, but Lauxhaul's committee expanded the event to include the seventh grade too, in addition to the eighth grade, because some of the committee members with daughters still in grade seven wanted their kids included as well. Why wait a whole year for their turn, they figured, when they had the chance to change the rules right now. They might have gotten away with it, too, if they hadn't bungled the food planning so thoroughly. With double the crowd, the committee arranged for only half the food they usually ordered. What used to be a leisurely morning munch for advancing girls and their grateful dads crumbled into a free-for-all grab for coffee, bland juice and a few meager muffins. The orange juice, I was told, had run out in the first few minutes. Naturally the parents picked sides.

My assignment this morning was to appease Lauxhaul. That's because the principal at the junior high believed too earnestly in the recuperative powers of psycho-counseling.

Therefore he had asked me to mediate. More likely he just didn't have the time or energy or desire to handle the scrum himself.

I hustled the hesitant Joan Petrochelli out of my office and felt grateful for at least a little lag time before Lauxhaul was due to arrive. Back at my desk I closed my eyes. I inhaled deeply. I anticipated the soothing sensation of quiet repose about to seep through me. But before it could my eyes snapped open again when voices from out at Tweed's desk grew suddenly harsh. I heard Tweed assert, "no, you absolutely can't go in there without an appointment. He's waiting for somebody else now anyway."

"But I only need a second," said the other. A woman. Linda.

"No, you absolutely can't go in there," Tweed repeated.

"But I have to see him," I heard Linda insist. "Just tell him it's me. It'll only take a second."

"It doesn't matter who you are. He can't see you now because he's expecting someone else."

"Just tell him it's Linda Winkle."

A charged silence ensued, electrically humming, twitching at eyelashes even where I sat, out of sight in another room. Tweed's voice finally broke through, rumbling low like a thunderclap.

"Did I hear you say your name is Linda Winkle," she tremored.

I shot up straight from my chair and scurried to the door. I got there just in time to see my ample secretary spring up from her own seat and sprint around her desk, screaming an incoherent, primitive screech as she ran, her hair dropping out of its orderly tuck, her eyes wide and wild and fixed savagely on Linda.

Trevor was out there too, lurking back by the entrance to the guidance department. The surprise from Tweed's ferocious onslaught made him slink back even farther. Linda stepped back too. Her mouth dropped open. She looked at Tweed in eye-popping surprise. Horror, even. Tweed's fulsome body slapped against Linda so forcefully that the younger woman slammed to the floor. Linda scrambled to get up, undamaged, angry, now showing a ferocious snarl of her own. By this time I reached Mrs. Tweed. I grabbed her arm. I thought a firm gesture would stop her. But Tweed wheeled around and swung her free hand with pinpoint accuracy to cuff me squarely in the face. I watched the blow coming, too surprised or maybe just too dumbwitted to avoid it, noticing her small, girl's fist as it came, her thumb clapped atop the curled edge of her index finger. An improper fist. My eyes flooded instantly with tears as the blow crashed against my nose. I reeled back reflexively in sudden blindness.

I blinked, blinked, blinked to regain my vision, stunned by the pain that rippled outward in fast circles from the bridge of my nose. I could hear the two women battling, their breathy oophs and yees and douphs, their feet scuffing for traction, their hands slapping against necks and faces, the thudding of more ponderous, body blows. Blurry through my tears and through the knife-point pain between my eyes I tried to see them. The guidance counselors were out of their offices now, hanging back close to their doors and making a wide ring around the flailing, dervishing women. Other people had rushed in too, running through the hallway of the administration wing, stopping in a knot of stunned and shocked onlookers who shrank back like the rest of us, not knowing what else to do. Tweed was getting the better of her, surprisingly, since she was a good twenty years older than Linda, and girthy. But she used her graceless bulk to her advantage, sticking out her gut and smothering it against Linda, blinking and ducking just slightly but otherwise ignoring the blows that Linda hailed upon her. After pinning Linda against the desk, Tweed snatched a fat handful of her hair and yanked it violently like a nag's halter until she forced Linda to double down at the waist. Then Tweed moved in for the kill, wedging Linda's head under her arm and locking it tight with her second arm, cinching tightly into a two-arm headlock and squeezing as if she wanted to pop off Linda's head like a champagne cork. Linda's face flashed crimson. She was done for.

Suddenly a man burst through the throng that had gathered from the hallway. He was unhesitant. He pried an arm between the two women – straining because Tweed held Linda so tightly – until he was able to lock both his arms around Mrs. Tweed's chest. He lifted her and shook, forcing her to let go of Linda. He set her down heavily on his other side, placing his own body resolutely between the battling women. It was Lauxhaul, who had just arrived for his appointment. I think he saved Linda's life.

I corralled Mrs. Tweed and Linda into my office and slammed shut the door. Linda retreated hastily to a far corner, terrified to be suddenly trapped in a room with her attacker. But Tweed was calm. In fact, she seemed almost serene.

"Are you crazy," I scolded her. "No, don't answer that. You really are crazy. Carmelita is one thing. That was something else. You attacked her out there. You know they'll never stand for violence. You're going to lose your job for that."

"Let them take it if they want," said Tweed unflustered. "She had it coming. She's probably had it coming for a long time. But I was the one to give it to her. No woman messes with the husband of Vivian Tweed."

"What are you talking about?"

"She's the one who made off with my Alfred."

"She did?"

"That's right. She did. Linda Winkle. When she told me her name just then I thought it was too good to be true. I thought, mine enemies hath been delivered up unto me. I knew I would get her someday. I just didn't think it would be this soon."

"But you just told me this morning that Alfred came back."

"That's right. He came back Saturday. He told me everything. That's how I know her name. I made him tell me. I told him that the only way I would take him back is if he tells me the whole story. Names, dates, places, everything. I made him tell me her name because I knew that someday I'd get the chance to get even. I just didn't think it would come this soon."

"But she couldn't have run off with your husband," I said to Tweed. "She's been going away to Atlantic City every weekend. I know because I've been watching . . . .."

Tweed raised an eyebrow. "You've been watching what?"

I looked across the room at Linda.

"I've been watching her son."

"Uh-huh," said Tweed. "And who do you think she's been going to Atlantic City with?"

I could not imagine Alfred Tweed as a high roller in the casinos of Atlantic City. And I could not picture Linda taking up with Alfred Tweed.

"But how could she," I asked Tweed incredulously still. "How could she run off with Alfred? He moved out. You told me that. You said he moved out of your house. But she's been here the whole time. It's only on the weekends she's been away."

"She's been here with him during the week and away with

him during the weekends. You thought you'd met up with a big-time sugar daddy, didn't you, honey," Tweed sniped at Linda. "You thought you were set for life. You can keep the damn money. We don't want it. We're better off without it. We'll take care of each other. But you," she looked Linda up and down contemptuously, "you'll piss through all that cash in a couple of months and then you'll be right back where you started: worthless. Worthless and alone."

"What money," I asked her. "What are you talking about?"

"The money she took from my Alfred. That's why he came back to me. He woke up Saturday morning and she was gone and the money was gone too. She stole it. He had this cheap fleabag room where he was keeping her and she snuck off with everything. That's the kind of woman she is. She steals from the man who puts her up. He puts her up and asks nothing in return – except maybe for a fast little tickle every other night or so. Or maybe every night if I know my Alfred. But I can't see why she'd mind that. She's nothing but a whore anyway."

"But what money," I persisted.

"The money he won. He won big this time, too. It was a long streak, I'll tell ya. He thought she was his good luck because she was there when it started. He went out to get some stamps from that machine at the little Quick Mart down on Roulston. Just plain ol' postage stamps. But then the sound of the coins dropping through the machine made him think of the slots. That's what he told me. I believe him too because I've seen it before. My father was the same way and you'd of thought I'd know better than to marry a man with a gambling addiction. But I did. And then this damn stamp machine gets him all whipped up at the Quick Mart. So he goes to the counter to buy a scratch ticket. Just one. At least that's what he told me. But wouldn't you know it he'd hit with that one ticket. Hit really big, too, he said. So he started yelling and shouting and dancing around. She just happened to be there at the same time, just buying cigarettes or something. Probably buying rubbers if I know her. He asked her out to breakfast because he said she must have been the good luck charm that made him win. He stopped for more tickets on the way and wouldn't you know it that he hit with some of those, too. He was up by a lot then. It was all over for him. There was no power on earth that could keep him out of the casinos after that."

"But how much money did he win?"

"He won a lot. He kept winning for a while at Atlantic City, too. But then it turned around. It always does. There wasn't much left. Only about twelve thousand dollars. That's what he told me. And you can have that, you bitch," Tweed shot over at Linda. "You won't get very far on that anyway. Not very far at all."

"Twelve thousand dollars," I repeated incredulously. "You're saying she took twelve thousand dollars from him?"

"You go ahead and keep the money," Tweed repeated. "I used to think I'd want all that money too but now it don't mean nothin' next to having my husband back. So you can have it if that's what it takes to keep you away from him. He won't be having anything to do with you now that you stole from him. So you go ahead and keep it. You won't get very far on it."

Still staying far away from Tweed, Linda leaned her full body weight against the wall and crossed her arms over her chest and glowered sullenly, a child caught at mischief. I just wanted her gone. But first I needed to move my secretary out of her path. I took Tweed by the elbow and turned her to face the door.

"Come on," I said to her hastily as I walked her toward the door. "We'll go over all this later. We'll have to figure out what we're going to do about all this. But first let me talk to Mrs. . . , to Mrs. . . .. " I stopped at the name, afraid the sound of Winkle might send Tweed on the attack once again. I gripped her arm more firmly, opened my office door, and whisked her out ahead of me as I finished the sentence. "Let me talk to Mrs. Winkle and get all of this straightened out with her. We'd better get her son in here too. Where's Trevor?"

In the reception area outside most of the people drawn by the fight had dispersed by now. I scanned the faces of the few who remained. I craned to see if maybe Trevor was standing behind someone. When I didn't see him I popped my head back into my office.

"Where's Trevor," I said to Linda.

She shrugged sullenly, looking unconcerned and detached and uncooperative.

"There's a boy who came in with her," I said to the others who were out by Tweed's desk. "Did anyone see where he went?"

They must have read some alarm in my voice. They looked one to the other. Alice, the skinny young counselor, and Edward, another guidance pro, stuck their heads into offices to see if maybe he had ducked into one. But Trevor was nowhere in our whole guidance suite. Edward and Alice paced quickly down the hall. In a moment Alice returned to tell me that some students in the adjoining high school had seen him flee from the building. They had watched him run down the long driveway from the school and our attached offices to the main road, where he'd hitched a ride. He'd gone left they said. But according to Alice, one student said she saw Trevor climb into a blue pickup, while another felt certain it was red car. But so what, I thought. I didn't have time to wade through the details Alice had gathered. I rushed back to my office for Linda.

"We have to go get him," I told her.

"I don't know where he went."

"He probably just went home. Come on. We have to go get him."

"I doubt if he went home."

"Just come on. We have to go find him."

CHAPTER THIRTEEN

I didn't trust her. I stayed close behind her as we rushed out through the reception area – me rushing because Trevor was already so many minutes ahead of us, Linda rushing, I suspected, simply to break away from me and get away. She glanced at me over her shoulder as she fled. I stayed tucked close behind her, until the superintendent of schools stepped suddenly in front of us and stuck out his hand like a crossing guard. Linda brushed past him but I had to stop. I stretched up on my toes to see overtop of him, watching Linda stride out away from me. When she looked back over her shoulder and saw that I had stopped, she stepped all the faster. I watched as she scooted down the hall and then disappeared around the corner that would lead her to the doors outside.

"What's going on in here," the superintendent demanded, straining for authority, tightening his chest to put resonance and reverberation in his voice .

"There was an incident involving a parent," I told him, choosing the word so loved by bureaucrats because is applied to everything without really describing anything – incident.

"A parent?" he repeated.

"A mother. From what I know so far she came here without an appointment. When she couldn't get in to see me she became agitated. She became violent and Mrs. Tweed had to get up and forcibly restrain her."

Tweed watched me keenly from her desk against the wall, right off my right shoulder. The others were watching too, the counselors and secretaries and hangers-on who had remained here after the fight, probably hanging on to hear a clear explanation themselves. I had been the first to arrive at the start of the fight, the only person to actually witness Tweed's opening assault. I realized that that none of the others could contradict me.

"For a moment I was concerned for Mrs. Tweed's safety," I said to the superintendent.

"Who is this woman," he asked me.

"She's the mother of one of our junior-high students. I've been seeing her son for a couple of weeks now. She's a very demanding woman."

"Are you all right," he asked Mrs. Tweed.

"I thought she did a very good job of defending herself," I said.

"I'm all right," Tweed told the superintendent.

"Is this something you think we should file charges over," he asked her.

She hesitated, watching me closely.

"I don't think so," she told him. "I took care of her. No harm was done."

"I have to go get the boy," I said to the school boss. "Her son is the one who left the school. I was just leaving with her to go find him now. I think I should go before he gets too far away. I can give you a complete report when I get back."

I hoped to get out to the lot in time to catch sight of Linda as she drove away. At least I would see which direction she turned, and maybe make a guess about where she was heading. And maybe, if all the intersections and the stoplights and the traffic lags broke in my favor, maybe I would even be able to catch up to her in my car. I burst out the doors and reared up in surprise when I saw Linda still sitting in her car in a handicapped parking space just outside the building. The car wasn't starting. Linda was turning the key. She pounded the steering wheel when she saw me come out. She turned the key more frantically. The Ford's big, tired V-8 engine cranked. It cranked and cranked. I walked slowly around to the door of the putty-colored cruiser. It cranked again. It wheezed. Linda released the key in frustration.

"Come on," I said through her open window. "We'll take my car."

The students who had watched Trevor leave the school had claimed he turned left out of the school driveway when he began to hitchhike away. But they couldn't even agree on what type car picked him up, so I ignored their report. I didn't want to waste any time following bad directions. I figured he must have turned right, because that was the direction that would take him back to Linda's apartment. I couldn't begin to guess where else he might go.

"With a little luck we might even catch him before he gets home," I said as we drove away in my car, gunning the gas to get the car quickly up to speed.

"He's not going home," said Linda, sullen in the seat beside me.

"Why not? Where else can he be going?"

"I don't know. But I know he's not going there."

"Why not?"

"Because it's not my apartment anymore."

I nudged the car onto the shoulder of the road and stopped, feeling a flash of anger stemming from confusion and hopelessness and even exhaustion. I let go of the steering wheel and turned in my seat toward Linda.

"What do you mean, it's not your apartment anymore?"

"I mean I gave it up."

"You gave it up?"

"I got my security deposit back this morning. I'm done. I handed in my keys. I can't even get in there anymore."

"So where are you living now?"

"I'm not living anywhere right now."

"But you've got to be living somewhere. Where is it? We'll go there to get Trevor."

"I said I don't have another place right now."

"Yes you do. You have to. Where is it? What, are you staying with some friends or something? Maybe with your family. Do your mother and father still live around here?"

"I'm not staying with anyone."

"You've got to be staying somewhere. What were you planning to do tonight? Sleep in your car?"

"I'm not a homeless, you know."

"Then where is your home?"

"I was just heading out."

"Heading out?"

"Yeah. Heading out. You know. Leaving town."

"You're leaving town? Well, where are you going?"

"I'm going to Florida. I'm going to get a place down there."

"Florida? Why Florida?"

"Because it's far away from here. That's why."

"Oh. I get it. You're on the run. So you really did take the money, didn't you?"

"No I didn't. Besides, why shouldn't I? It's my money too. We won it together on all those trips down to Atlantic City. He was just going to gamble it all away again anyway. I could see that coming a mile away. At least I've got enough God-damned sense to get the hell out of there. She never did. She can have him now. He'll never win that much money again."

"That's the only reason you moved in with him, isn't it? To get the money."

"I didn't plan it that way, if that's what you mean. Besides, I only kind of half moved in with him."

"Half moved in? How can you half move in? He left his wife for you. He wouldn't have done that unless he thought he was getting something better. Besides, I saw you moving. I didn't realize it at the time, but now I do. That's why you were carrying all your clothes out to your car the time I brought Trevor back after that first weekend. Remember? The time you ditched me behind Wal-mart. That's where you were going. You were moving all your clothes to wherever you were staying and you didn't want me to know about it."

"Those weren't all my clothes. Like I said, I never moved in all the way. I kept the other place too. That's where me 'n Trevor lived. I couldn't very well take him to live with me 'n Al, now could I?"

"You expect me to believe that you were living in two places at once?"

"I don't care what you believe, but that's what I was doing."

"That's impossible."

"I told him I had a job. That I had to go to work every day. That's when I went back to my other place."

"Didn't he get a little suspicious?"

"He's not that smart."

"You never even told him that you have a son, either, did you? He never even knew it, did he? That's why you kept dropping Trevor off with me. So he wouldn't find out."

"Men don't like women once they know they have children."

"Oh come on. You don't think he took you for some fresh young bimbo or something, do you? You're not, you know."

"I'm as young a bimbo as he'll ever get."

"So you only let him think you were living with him until you found out where he stashed the money. Is that it?"

"I didn't have to find out where. I knew where. He trusted me."

"And this is how you repay him? By robbing him blind? I hope you at least left him a little."

"Why? He would of only gambled it all away again, like I already said. I just got out of there before it was too late. I didn't plan it like this. And I'll tell you another thing: it's a lot more money than what he told her. A lot more. She might think he told her everything, but if he told her there was only twelve thousand left then she doesn't know the whole story."

"How much more?"

"A lot more. Enough for me to live off of for a long time and not have to worry about anything. I never had this much money in my life."

"Where is it?"

Reflexively she clutched her handbag tighter, both hands cinching its top snugly as she tucked it close to her gut. If the bills were large enough, the purse could carry quite a bundle.

"It must be some wad," I said.

As we sat parked beside the road cars raced past us furiously, the buildup to noontime traffic. The lunch crowd. The shopping crowd. The anonymity of automobiles. Maybe some of them were dashing away to Florida too. I watched in my rearview mirror for a traffic gap large enough to let me re-enter.

"We'd better go find Trevor so the two of you can get out of here," I said to her. I added absently, "the schools aren't very good down in Florida, you know."

"He's gonna stay here."

"What? Trevor? He's gonna stay here?"

"He has to. I don't even have a place to live down there yet."

"But where is he going to stay," I queried. Then I got it. I said, "oh, I see. That's why you came to my office this morning. That's why you brought him along. You were going to leave Trevor with me."

"It's just for a while. Until I get settled. I gotta find an apartment. And I want to get a job, too. Not a big job. But I want to make maybe just a little bit of money to pay at least some of my bills. Then I can make what I got now last a whole lot longer."

"You mean like a waitress at a diner or something?"

"Yeah, something like that."

"It sounds like a halfway decent plan," I confessed. "Except the part about leaving your son behind."

"It's just for a while. Then I'm going to send for him. Maybe I'll even fly him down in an airplane. He's never flown in an airplane before."

"Why not just take him with you now?"

"I can't. Not until I'm settled in. There's some people I

know down there. I'm going to stay with them till I get every-thing set up. They wouldn't want him around."

"Does Trevor know all this?"

"I told him on the way over. We hugged and said goodbye in the parking lot before we came in."

"That explains why he took off."

"Everything would of been all right if that bitch hadn't jumped me."

"Where do you think he's going?"

"I don't know."

"Well then think of the places he might go. We'll drive to all of them until we find him."

"All of them? There's about a million."

"Then let's start with the most likely ones first."

She led me to the urban core, to a street I'd never been near before because it was deep-city territory where people from my suburban neighborhood just don't go. I wedged the car along-side the curb in front of a three-decker house of stacked flats that was clad in dingy yellow siding, vinyl slats that were pocked with stone-sized holes and brittle fissures. Outside, on the porch of the street-level flat, a man wearing slippers and bathrobe sat passively on a stuffed couch that was too long for the porch. It reached past the door that led inside the apartment. You would have to step awkwardly around the old couch to squeeze inside the front door. I checked my car door to make sure it was locked and I walked around to Linda's side to check that the passenger door was locked too.

"It's all right," Linda said. "It's never as bad as you think around here."

I hustled to get abreast of her as she started down the sidewalk. We passed a lanky youth in drooping jeans who had his head stuck under the open hood of a pickup. A young woman watched him from the curb beside the truck, shapely, smooth-skinned in her youth, standing barefoot beside the spill of the young man's tools on the ground. She held a little tot propped on a hip that she jutted sideways to support the child. He was bare below a spotted tee-shirt, his legs plump and his small toes splayed and pudgy. Was she his sister, I wondered, or could the young girl be the little tot's mother? Linda turned suddenly and cut up a narrow walk that led between two of the tall, boxy three-deckers that lined the street. The houses here were packed closely together, with only the concrete walkway spanning the gap between the two houses. It was a narrow sidewalk at that. Before we entered the passage between the two buildings, Linda and I had to stop and wait for a man walking toward us. As he approached he nodded and grinned as if he knew us. Linda ignored him. Instead she stared at a makeshift gate nailed awkwardly to one of the houses and closing the sidewalk ahead of us.

"Don't worry at all about that," said the man as he approached, grinning wider now from the engagement. "Frank he just put that up just the other day. Just about two days ago. We just got it there so the dog can't git out anymore." He pushed the gate open and held it for us as we passed. Linda ignored him still as we brushed past the man.

She led me around to the back of one tall, shabby house to where concrete steps led down to a basement doorway recessed under a back porch. She pressed a doorbell and then pounded on the door, yelling, "Andy, Andy, are you in there?"

"Come on," she said to me after she tried the knob and pushed open the door. "I think he's here. He's gotta be here."

We entered a basement apartment, dimly lit by a couple of squat windows stuck high on the inside walls. Linda reached and flipped up a switch near the door. A naked bulb in a ceiling fixture flashed bravely and threw a pale yellow glare. We stood in the kitchen, I guessed. A table near us had an open space cleared on its top, large enough to set a single meal. All around the space on the table top lay a jumble of unopened mail, two books, a give-away tabloid of entertainment listings, seven or so empty beer bottles, a cap, a coffee mug, a sweater heaped in a pile, an artsy small pamphlet, a cereal box, a hand trowel, an ashtray brimmed with dirty-white ash flecks and crushed cigarette ends. On a countertop near the table stood a cube-shaped dorm refrigerator, a hotplate, an electric frying pan, a corded tea kettle and a package of Chips Ahoy. No stove. A broom leaned against a wall and low down next to it sat a dustpan. Pale, patterned linoleum on the floor was rutted down to the concrete beneath it where feet had etched paths in front of the countertop and approaching the doorways. All around us the air seemed stained with the scent of cigarette smoke pierced through by acrid jabs of solvent or oil.

"I'm in here," called a voice weighted low by sleep. Linda moved through a door that led deeper into the cellar apartment. I stepped close behind her. In the next room I could make out a man groping to sit up on the couch where he had just been asleep. I saw shoulder-length hair.

"It's me," said Linda.

"Oh. Yeah." He rubbed fingers over his eyes and blinked.

"We're looking for Trevor."

"Turn on that light," he said.

Linda waved her hand into the blank air in front of her and found the pull-string dangling from a ceiling light. The bulb flashed on abruptly. Andy sat hunched on the couch. He squeezed his eyes shut and opened them slowly. He looked at Linda in dim comprehension. He turned his whole head slow like a reptile to gaze at me standing right beside her.

"This is my friend Dan," she said to him. "He drove me because my car's not working."

"What's wrong with it this time?" The words seeped out.

"I don't know. It's just old. I'm gonna get a new one soon."

He stretched slowly, ungracefully, an awkward movement that most people would never perform in the presence of others. Andy wore thick corduroy trousers and a knit cardigan over an old herringbone vest over a shirt. I wondered if maybe his apartment felt cold. I looked at a large wooden easel across the room that held a big panel of hardboard, a painting in progress. It was large, maybe three feet wide by five feet tall, so that the woman in the painting looked life-size. Beside the easel stood a tall kitchen stool cluttered with curled paint tubes, brushes, pigment smears and a solvent jar. Other paintings leaned in a jumble in the corner behind the easel. Most were on canvas on stretchers, I thought, though I couldn't see them clearly through the disorder.

"You're a painter," I said suddenly.

"He used to be," said Linda. From the couch Andy bent and reached toward a low freighter trunk that served as a coffee table in front of him. He found a crumpled cello-pack and dug inside it for a cigarette. "He doesn't really do much anymore," Linda went on. When she followed my eyes to the unfinished painting of the woman across the room, she said, "wow. Who is that? What are you painting her for?"

"What? That? That's the lady who runs some damn New Age church a couple blocks from here. I can never remember what she calls it. The Church of . . . no, The Center for . . . phhht, I don't remember. It's something like that. I've been going there. She tells me I should do these spiritual portraits. That's what that is. It's supposed to be when you connect with their spiritual nature or some bullshit and paint that instead of what they really look like. I don't know. It's all a bunch of bullshit. She says I can make money at it. That's why I've been going there. To her church, I mean. To sell portraits to them. But nobody wants one. They're all a bunch of rich hypocrites from the suburbs. They come down here once a week for this church that she's running. They must think it's daring. They really don't want to have anything to do with me. I don't even know why they go there. It's not like it's a real church. It's more like it's a game for them. They need to have something. I think I scare them off."

"What are you going to do with it," I asked him.

"What? The painting? I don't know. I have to finish it. She gave me two-fifty for it. But I'm not going to give it to her for that. Not for two hundred and fifty bucks."

The woman in the painting appeared suspended, floating in a lightly colored burst of what might be a cloud or a shock of electromagnetism or spectral uncertainty or who knew what. Her body was wrapped in a gauzy reveal that still displayed all of her sensuous flesh. Her breasts. She had three arms, with the third arm curling to the foreground from behind her back and thrusting forward her hand with the palm turned up, asking. I took the woman to be charismatically attractive. I took the painting to be very good.

"She just wants to make money off me," said Andy. "She says when I finish it there'll be lots of other people she knows that want one done. She says she'll help me sell 'em to all the people that go to her church. But I'm just gonna tell her I can't do it. It's too much bullshit. They don't want to have anything to do with me anyway. I scare them too much. Do you want a beer?"

Andy paused and took a long pull from a Heineken can that sat open amid all the other clutter on the trunk by his couch.

"We need to find Trevor," said Linda. "We thought he might of come here."

"Where is he?"

"I don't know where he is. He took off. That's why we're looking for him."

"He didn't come here. I haven't seen Trevor in, phhht, I don't know. He doesn't come here anymore."

Linda looked back at the painting. "Are you fucking her," she asked him.

"Her? She doesn't want to have anything to do with me. She just wants to make some money off me. Use me to do some portraits for her people, her church people, for her . . . whatever they are."

"From that painting it looks to me like you're fucking her," Linda said.

From the painting I thought that he probably wouldn't need to. I thought that maybe the painting alone was intimacy enough.

"She doesn't care about me," he repeated. He groped for another cigarette from the crumpled cello-pack on the trunk. After he lit it he looked up at Linda and said, "what kind of car are you going to get?"

"I don't know. One that works."

As we left he asked Linda for money to buy more ciga-rettes. When she turned him down he put the question straight to me. I dug three dollars from my wallet.

When we were back in my car Linda said to me, "you know, three dollars isn't enough to buy a pack of cigarettes now."

"It isn't?"

"Not anymore. Not for a long time."

"I didn't know," I said.

After a moment I asked her, "why would Trevor have gone there?"

"We used to live there."

"With Andy?"

"We used to be married," she said.

"You were married to Andy?"

"He wasn't always like that," she said. "Or if he was like that I didn't mind it as much at the time."

"But what makes you think this is the first place Trevor would go to?"

"Where else would he go? Trevor likes Andy. They always got along real good together. When Trevor was little Andy used to play with him like he was a little kid himself. He used to get down on the floor and play with toy dinosaurs and little soldiers and all that kind of stuff. It was like Trevor had a playmate his own age, except it was Andy. Then, when Trevor got a little older, if I wasn't around for a while he started doing things for Andy. Like picking up and answering the phone and getting the mail. Little things like that. Then it was the opposite. It was like Andy had an adult his own age to help him, except it was Trevor."

"Is Andy Trevor's father," I asked her.

"No," she said dismissively. I wanted to ask her more, to see if her answer could be trusted. But before I could speak again she pointed to a curb-side spot where I could park. We had landed at our next destination.

This neighborhood was far different from Andy's, although it wasn't too far distant. The area was hipper, tonier, and even a little cleaner than Andy's triple-decker district. It showed some bohemian sheen. A small, grassy, treed park split two streets. There were small restaurants here, and a cappuccino place. There was a florist, a bike shop, a book store, a pastry shop and a framery. There was a square brick building called the Pregnancy Crisis Center. An Episcopalian church stood near a funeral home that had taken over a big old house. My car was in front of a plain apartment cube that stood a few stories high. Linda walked to the entrance and rang at the bank of buttons near the door. She rang a specific apartment. I expected a query to come through the intercom, a simple "who is it." Instead we were buzzed in at once.

Linda led me up one flight and clear to the end of the second-floor hallway to the last apartment. The door was standing fully open and held with a magazine doubled and wedged under its bottom. In the living room a woman asleep on a couch wore just a bra and panties that showed from the bedsheet that was thrashed and twisted around her. A second woman stepped in from the kitchen, inquisitive. She held a fork in her hand. She chewed. A third came in from an inner hallway, closing her bathrobe when she saw me. Her hair was wet from the shower. Linda looked from one woman to the next. She stuck her hands in her pockets.

"This is Dan," Linda announced. To me she said, "that's Gretchen and that's Honey. And this is Tif on the couch."

Tif stretched out a leg and kicked it to shake loose the twisted sheet. She opened her eyes slowly and looked at us.

"This is Dan," Linda repeated to her.

"You can't bring him here," the woman in the bathrobe, Honey, said to her. "This isn't a damn hotel, you know. He can spring for a room."

"He's a friend of mine," Linda answered.

"You must be one hard-up, horny guy, comin' here with her like this," Honey sneered toward me. "Why don't you just spring for a room?"

"We came here looking for Trevor," Linda said. "He took off again."

"Good for him," said Honey, who then turned and disappeared down the hallway.

"What makes you think he'd come here," Gretchen asked her.

"I don't know where he went. I'm just checking out a lot of different places."

"Well, he's not here."

Tif sat up on the couch. She blinked her eyes. She was still fogged from sleep. She asked Linda, "did you move back here?"

"I'm not back," Linda said.

"You can't bring him here," Tif said. "That's one of our rules. Remember?"

"I'm not bringing him here," Linda answered. "He's a friend. We went to high school together. He's helping me find Trevor."

"Oh," Tif replied. "Where's Trevor?"

"I don't know where he is," Linda answered. "That's why I'm looking for him. That's why we came here."

Tif stood up from the couch. She shook free the bedsheet and opened it wide to wrap the sheet across her chest and clench it under her armpits before she sat down again. Tif was the youngest among the roommates, still in her twenties, I guessed.

"You should of called or something," she said to Linda.

"There wasn't any time for that. We're trying to catch up to Trevor."

"Well you still should of called. We would of told you he's not here. Instead of just barging in like this. You already know that I sleep out here."

"We just came in for a minute, just to see if he's here."

"How would you like it if I just barged into your bedroom when you were asleep?"

"I didn't know you'd be sleeping now."

"You know when I work."

"No I don't. Not anymore. I haven't been here for a long time. Things change, you know."

From across the room Gretchen said to me, "we're students," not caring about how unlikely that sounded.

"I can't believe you just barge in here like this," Tif went on.

"I didn't barge in," answered Linda. "I rang the bell."

"Well I didn't buzz you in," said Tif.

"I did," flipped Gretchen.

"It's not like you live here anymore or anything," stewed Tif.

"She sleeps out here 'cause we only have two bedrooms," Gretchen confided to me. She was sizing me up, watching me as Linda and Tif quibbled back and forth, assessing my size, my shape, my features, my clothing, my hair, my general demeanor and bearing. She took me to be Linda's man, I guessed. She was wondering, was I a good catch? Was I worth her envy? Could she steal me if she wanted to? Would I be worth her bother? Could she do even better?

"Now I'll never get back to sleep," Tif complained.

"I said I was sorry," Linda said.

"Honey's got the room that used to be Linda's," Gretchen told me. She paused to push her tongue against her teeth, digging at a stuck morsel. "I got the biggest room," she said. "Come on. I'll show ya."

"You never think of anyone but yourself," Tif groused at Linda.

"I didn't know you'd be sleeping now," Linda answered.

Gretchen started down the hallway, then stopped to look back to see if I was following. She reached a finger into her mouth to flick at the morsel with a nail.

At last Linda said, "I don't have time for this bullshit." She grabbed my arm and pulled me toward the propped-open door. With her foot she scuffed away the bent magazine so the door would swing closed.

"If you don't want people to come in here you should keep this God damn door shut," she shouted backward as she rushed me out of the apartment.

From there we traveled out to a suburb of houses medium in size but older and well anchored, set inside trim green yards well tended and showing off aristocratic airs. Linda pointed me into a driveway, where I parked behind a Buick sport-utility vehicle. She told me that Trevor had spent some time here as a foster child. The woman who came to front door looked surprised.

"Jonathan," she called inside, "Jonathan, come see who's here."

Jonathan was bearded, the type who wears whiskers as a shield of airy intellectualism. He approached curiously, then stopped a few steps back from the screen door, gazing out at us from over his wife's shoulder.

"Oh," he exclaimed simply. His wife reached up to check the little lock on the handle of the screen door that separated us.

"This is my friend, Dan," Linda announced. "He's a psychiatrist too."

"Psychologist," I corrected.

Jonathan tipped a little to the side to get a better view of me. I could scarcely make him out behind his wife in the shadow behind the screen door. The woman looked me up and down with intensity. She talked past Linda, saying to me, "I don't know why you're bringing her here. I don't want anything to do with her. I've already been through it all and I'm not going to put up with any more of it."

"Besides," she went on after a long breath, "this is my day off. I'm not working today. I keep normal office hours. You have to make an appointment. I don't know why you ever would have brought her here anyway. This is my home."

"Oh," I said, "so you're the psychologist."

"Of course I am. Who did you think I was?"

"We're not coming here to see you," Linda said.

"If you need to consult with me, fine. We can always do that. But on a professional basis. Not here at my home. I don't know why you brought her here to my home. This is highly unorthodox."

"He's just helping me look for Trevor," Linda said.

"I can't tell you anything about her anyway," Jonathan's wife said to me, speaking past Linda. "I never really saw her in any sort of official capacity. When her son was here with us in the foster program I saw her coming and going a lot, but that was all. That's all I think I could stand."

"We just want to know if he's been here," Linda said.

"But this is very unorthodox, don't you think? I mean, coming here to my home like this. And bringing her along besides. Why didn't you just call my office? What ever made you think you could come to my home? What made you think I'd be home in the first place? You're lucky to catch me here."

"Linda brought me here."

She looked us up and down again. "I don't understand. What for?"

"We're trying to find Trevor," I said. "There was a . . . a . . . er . . . an incident this morning at my office and he left. We're going to all the different places we think he might be."

"What kind of an incident?"

"What kind? It was an argument, I guess. But that's not important right now," I said. "What's important is that Trevor slipped out and nobody knows where he went. Linda brought me here to see if we could find him."

"I'm not surprised," said the woman. "I don't know where he's been since he left us but if he's been back with her it's a wonder she's kept him this long. Have you reported it?"

"Reported it? To who?"

"Well to Child Protective Services, of course. You have to report it to them. They already have quite a file on these two. They'll probably want to take custody again. Good luck to them. I won't have him back here."

"But he just left," I explained. "This all just happened this morning. He's barely been gone and it wasn't a big deal. The incident, I mean. It was more of a simple misunderstanding. And it didn't involve Trevor and Linda anyway. Not the both of them. It's just that Trevor slipped out and now we want to find him. That's all. It's nothing so serious that we need to call Protective Services. I've been involved for some time, officially, so I'm in a better position to judge. I don't think this is so serious that I'd call Protective Services."

"It sure looks serious to me," she said. "What, with you coming out here personally in the middle of the afternoon. And bringing his mother besides. I'd never do anything like that. Don't you think it's a bad idea to get so personally involved? If it was me I'd call Child Protective Services. They'll find him and then they'll take the appropriate actions."

"I can handle it better than that," I said. "And I'm not so sure that child services would take such appropriate actions."

"What do you mean," she wondered. "Of course they would. That's their job. Besides, they're the authorities here. Especially in cases like this. They're probably the only ones left who can do anything here. He ran away from us too, you know."

"No, I didn't know that."

"Last year."

"Why," I asked her.

"The usual reasons. He didn't like it that we expected some things out of him. Like he had to be home after school, couldn't go certain places, things like that. It's not completely his fault. He never had any kind of order and structure in his life. Because of her. She even influenced him when he was here. You know, told him he didn't have to do certain things. Maybe she even told him he should run away from us. It would be so much better if they just didn't permit any contact at all with the biological parent."

"Maybe he just didn't like you," Linda cut in.

"Just look at where he comes from," said the psychologist. "She's a prostitute, you know."

"I know."

"Not anymore," shot Linda.

"You would think that after having one child that she can't take care of, you would think she'd at least change her ways a little."

"I only did that for a while," said Linda.

"Obviously you haven't seen Trevor today," I said to the woman.

"And I can take care of my son just fine," Linda went on.

"If I had seen him, I would have called the proper authorities right away. In fact, I'll call them right now if you'd like me to. They'll probably find him a lot faster than you will."

"No," I insisted. "I don't mind doing it myself. I really think it's better this way. In fact, if you don't mind, I'd like to ask you as a professional courtesy that you not report it. I'm the closest to this right now, and I really think that it's best this way. At least for now. I understand your point of view, but I'd like to ask that you not report it."

"Okay," she replied. "Have it your way."

I figured she would report it anyway, which made me more desperate to find him. If I had him present and beside me, I could maybe pry loose the piercing claws the care agency sinks into a kid. I could tell them the woman's call was a misunderstanding. I could tell them that Trevor was safe with his appointed guardian, his mother, right here in front of me and under my guidance. Maybe they'd buy that and drop the whole thing. Maybe. Or maybe not. Once a kid's name appears on the top of a form, the state child-care controllers behave like they jealously own him.

I drove with Linda to two other households. The afternoon grew stale and slanted. Linda demanded to check the last few possibilities by phone. She insisted I stay in the car while she camped at a sooty pay phone outside a doughnut shop to make the calls. She might have been phoning anyone, making any sort of arrangement. She returned to the car frowning. He was gone.

CHAPTER FOURTEEN

It was long dark by the time Linda and I started back toward the school. She felt convinced that her car would start now, as if all it had needed was a long, quiet rest. I tried consoling myself by thinking that at least she couldn't get away to Florida in the limping wreck. She would have to stay here at least a few days longer to get it fixed or maybe buy another. But who was I kidding? The car wouldn't keep Linda. She might even turn south tonight and drive deep into the darkness, maybe just to get away as far as she could from me before the engine fagged again. She assured me she wouldn't. She told me she planned to spend the night with friends. She would find Trevor in the morning, she said, and she would call me at my office when she did.

"I promise," she added for extra assurance.

But we had already been to visit all of her friends. She didn't know anyone who would put her up for the night. I saw that too clearly to delude myself anymore. Reluctantly I confronted the fact that these last few moments here in my car, right now during this sullen drive back to her stuttering auto, this awkward trip was my last chance to ask her my one probing question about the boy. As we paced out the last few miles to the school we seemed to be the only two people still out on the streets. Darkness wrapped our car. I stared ahead grimly through the windshield, watching with dread for the gaudy, glowing sulfur halo of lights that surrounded the high school to loom through the darkness ahead of us. There wouldn't be time after that. Before they appeared I asked her abruptly, "so, who is Trevor's father?"

Linda turned her head and looked long at me, but she did not answer.

"It's just that our visit to your ex-husband today got me thinking about it. Especially since, you know, especially since when you first came in to see me you said that he was, you know, you said that I was his father."

After a simmering pause she asked me, "do you want the truth?"

"Of course I want the truth."

"The truth is I don't really know who his father is."

"But how can you not know something like that?"

"I just don't. That's all. Those were some wild times back then. You remember: the hippie days, with free love and free sex and women's liberation and communes and everything else like that."

"But you have to have some idea. You said today that Andy isn't his father. It sounded like you knew that for sure. If you know for sure that someone's not his father, you must have an idea who his father is."

"I guess I have an idea. Yeah. But so what?"

"So, well, it's just something I want to know."

"There's a few people it could be."

"When you said I was his father you were making that up, weren't you?"

"Yeah. Well, kind of. You could be his father."

"But you don't think I am?"

"No. I don't think you are."

"Then who else?"

She looked at me silently. Gauging me. Sizing me. Scheming somehow. I grew more anxious. I grew impatient with her silence. Ahead of us the first brilliant stab of skyward light from the school lot appeared.

"I don't see why you want to know so bad," she said.

"I'm not sure why myself."

"If you think maybe you can find out who his father is and get him to take Trevor or maybe pay for child support or something, forget it. That would never work."

"That's not it at all," I said. "I just want to know. For my own sake. For my own satisfaction."

"I'm just not sure. There's two or three people it might be. It might even be your father."

We were inside the lot, fully washed and bleached pale by the big lights above us even as we sat in the car. I rolled my auto abreast of Linda's sagging Ford as it waited with ageless patience in the handicapped spot where she had abandoned it earlier. It looked rooted, the only car left in the lot. I turned off my engine and felt the stillness possess us as my mind engaged the words just spoken by Linda. It might even be your father. She made no movement to climb out.

"Is this something else you're making up," I asked her.

"Because if it is, you don't need to, because after today you should already know that I'm willing to look out for him. I don't need some kind of connection, if that's what you're trying to do."

"I didn't know he was in the house that time we, well, you know, that one time you got together with me. God, that was so many ages ago. It seems like forever now but I still remember it real bright and clear. You must of saw him or something because you just jumped off the bed and ran out. Remember? All the sudden you were gone. I didn't know why. I thought maybe you just lost your nerve or something. I didn't know what to do. When you didn't come back after a few minutes I got up to go look for you. I didn't put my clothes on or anything because I thought we were still all alone in the house. I thought we were still, you know, still doin' it. I thought maybe you just needed some extra convincing or something to finish me off. So I went out to find you. I was naked and everything. Completely. I went down the hall and walked right into a room. It was the first room I came to. I guess I must of heard someone in there. I must of thought it was you. I ran in fast like you were hiding and we were playing hide 'n seek or something. You know, like we were teasing each other or something. I felt so stupid. I got all the way to the middle of the room before I stopped all the sudden because I saw it wasn't you in there. I figured right away it had to be your father. At least he was embarrassed too. I turned around to get out of there as fast as I could but he called me right back. And I went back, too. It was weird. It was like, I don't know, it was different. I can't describe it. Usually I would of just kept running till I was long gone out of there. I mean, I wasn't wearing any clothes or anything. But I stopped before I got out of the room and I turned around to see what he wanted. I wasn't wearing a thing. At least he was embarrassed too. He said he wanted to sketch me. He said he was an artist and he never got a chance like this and he wanted to use it now and not let it get away. I'd never heard anybody say they were an artist before. The room we were in was like a painter's studio or something, with paints and paper and big paintings all over the place. He was embarrassed by the whole thing too and I figured he had to mean what he said. I mean, you hear guys say things like that all the time, like they just want to take your picture and that's all. But I knew this wasn't just a big come-on line. I don't know how. I just knew it. It was like, I don't know, it was like I knew he could see something in me. Like I was beautiful or something. He didn't say that. But I could feel it for sure. The whole thing was so different. Everything. It was just so different. He laid out a sheet or a tarp or something like that on the floor, but then he picked it back up again and he went out of the room and he came back with a pad or a thin mattress or cushion or something and he laid that down. He put the sheet back down on top of that and then I laid down on it without ever saying a word. He went back over by the big window where he'd been sitting when I ran in and he started to draw me with a pencil. I don't know how long it took because I really wasn't paying any attention to time, I felt so comfortable and everything. I felt like I could stay there forever, like I was getting some kind of a super massage or hot bath or a pedi or I don't know what. I didn't want it to ever end. I didn't care that I was naked. I didn't even know it anymore. He just sat there drawing me without ever saying anything. When he was finished he came over and showed it to me. I said wow or something stupid like that and then I just sat there looking at it for a while. I didn't know what to do so I just kept looking at his picture without saying anything. I don't think he knew what to do either because he just stayed there crouched down beside me holding it out so I could see it. After a couple of minutes of that he got down on the pad and fucked me. It was, like, the most natural thing that could ever happen. It was like it was in the stars or something. Like it was the only thing that could ever happen right then for either one of us. The only thing we could do. So it just happened. The perfectly natural thing."

All the times I had wondered how Linda had found her way out of my house, that was the only possibility I never could have imagined. In a moment she said, "after that we both knew we were done. He gave me the picture when I was leaving."

"Was it good," I asked her.

"I thought it was good. I thought it was real good. I really liked it. I thought it was real good and I thought it looked just like me. But when I started taking up with Andy, he said it wasn't any good at all."

"Do you have it still?"

"No. Andy wrecked it. He drew over it and it wasn't any good after that so I just threw it away. Actually, I burned it. My parents used to burn their old palms when they got new ones on Palm Sunday. They burned them instead of just throwing them away because the palms were blessed so you didn't want them just in with the trash. So that's what I did. I burned it."

"And you think you got pregnant then? I mean, you think my father is Trevor's dad?"

"He could be. I don't know. There's a few people it could be. It's not just him."

"But didn't you ever try to find out? Don't you want to know?"

"How? You mean with tests or something?"

"Yeah. You could do that."

"No. I don't want to know."

"But why not?"

"Because I'm afraid it might turn out not to be him."

She sat silently, taking whole minutes to absorb and accept her own statement. I guessed that this was the first time she ever had said it, and as such it was also the first time she ever had fully acknowledged the fact. She wanted to believe that her son was special. I thought to ask her why, if she attached that value to Trevor, why was she abandoning him. But I couldn't interrupt the silence with a question that Linda never would honestly answer anyway. In her view she wasn't abandoning Trevor. She was simply doing something that she had to do. Like scratching an itch.

When finally she opened the door to climb out of my car, the sound pierced the silence like a rifle crack. At her own car the door made a sturdy clunk when she tugged it shut. The automobile started right up, obedient to Linda's whim. Its engine shuddered and hissed as she gunned the gas one time, two times, three times to test its sincerity. Her transmission clunked into reverse and she began to back out of the space. She could have pulled straight ahead because there was no car parked in front of hers. The whole lot was empty except for my silent auto beside her. But instead she backed away from the space and away from my car. Her tires scuffed the asphalt as she turned the steering wheel to point her auto toward the exit. Her transmission clunked again as it dropped into a forward gear. The engine hissed and groaned and finally worked toward a grumble as Linda urged the rusting, rattling hulk away from me. I raised my eyes and watched in my rearview mirror as her taillights receded. The twin red lights shrank smaller. They shrank to mere dots and then veered out of sight at the end of the lot where Linda turned away.

CHAPTER FIFTEEN

I coaxed myself home – to my parents' home again – feeling sagged and exhausted. I slept solidly that night, nothing at all like the fitful, restless sleep I had endured the first night I'd returned to this house of my childhood. I awoke the next morning in the midst of a dream. A ship's captain had given command of his vessel to me just before he flopped over the top railing into the sea, while the people above deck applauded. In the phantom lapse of a dream I next found myself low down in the bowels of the ship. I stood with Elizabeth, my mother. Her memories were restored and her mind was whole. She looked happy. She laughed. A warm smile stayed broad on her face. Then a man standing in the feathery room with us, a kind of watchman, it seemed, told me politely to leave because now, he said, he had to lock up. I wanted Elizabeth to come along with me but the man insisted she stay. I complained that she would be all alone in the vacant space, but the man assured me that she was okay. She was happy down here, he told me. So I climbed out alone and the people above deck applauded.

Well, dream or no dream, at least I had slept. As I laid in bed in the dimness, I consoled myself still more with the thought that this morning my father wasn't standing like a specter in the bedroom doorway, like I had found him yesterday. In fact, come to think of it, I hadn't heard a stir from my father the whole night. Not even when I slipped in the door and crept up to my bedroom late in the evening after the frustrated search to find Trevor. My dad should have been waiting and nervously clamoring to convince me that I just couldn't stay. That the situation here was too bad. That I had no idea what he was going through. But he'd been asleep himself. And soundly asleep too, I guessed, because throughout the whole night I hadn't even heard my father turn in his bed. Certainly that helped explain why I had slept so well myself.

I felt glad he had left me alone. The day now crouching ahead of me already brimmed with obstacles enough. Trevor was still on the loose. Where on earth would I find him? When would I even have a moment to look? At work I would have to somehow explanation yesterday's fight between Linda and Tweed to the big boss, the superintendent. That was on top of my regular appointments. I would have plenty of those, to boot. I had skipped out on the whole day's schedule when I had dashed off to find Trevor yesterday morning. Plus another full caseload waited on the books for today. I showered, dressed, and slipped out to my car without hearing a murmur from my father. He was sleeping quite soundly indeed.

Still, I arrived at my office late that morning. I closed my door for a few moments alone to brace for the onslaught I expected. But instead of the school superintendent demanding an explanation for yesterday's brawl, instead of a buzz from Tweed to tell me that a sniveling teen had arrived for counseling, the first noise to disturb me was a telephone call from timid Mrs. Hodges, a neighbor who lived near my parents.

Speaking in a nervous flutter through the phone, Mrs. Hodges reminded me that she had jotted my office number once to keep as a precaution, a daytime emergency contact. She apologized. I told her there was no need. She said she would not bother me at work unless it was absolutely necessary. I told her I knew that. She said the only reason she had called me now was because it was an emergency. Okay, I got that, I said. I had the impression she was reading from a sheet, as if she had written down in advance what to say. She told me she was at my parents' house. There were some people there with her, and after she had fetched my number for them they had said it would be better for her to call first. To get me on the line, she said. People? I asked her, what people? I heard her pass over the phone.

It was a police officer, who had arrived with the ambulance that was summoned by the fisherman who had found my father's body lifeless in the three-acre pond out beyond the woods behind my parents' house that morning.

CHAPTER SIXTEEN

On the face of it there was nothing extraordinary about my father drowning in the pond near his house this morning. He swam there all the time. Or at least he used to. Before this year, he used to swim every day in late spring, summer and into the fall. Swimming was his chief recreation, and he observed the same ritual day after day for year after year. Every morning he hiked the half mile or so back to the secluded small lake. He stripped down to his boxers and swam the full length across and then back in his slow loping stroke, like a frog except that he held his head high above water. Back on the shore he peeled off the soaked boxers and wrung them in a knot. He slipped on his outer clothes, which he had left folded and dry on the water's edge. He carried the wet, knotted shorts at his side as he walked back home.

But this year he had not returned to the ritual. Elizabeth made it impossible, he had told me. He couldn't leave her alone.

He couldn't even leave her unwatched in another room, he had raged at me. No way could he ever walk down to the pond and swim its full length and walk back with my mother alone in the house. So he had given up swimming, apparently until just this morning.

When I arrived the livingroom was crowded with the policemen, the firemen and the ambulance crew who had left their bold vehicles in a rapid hash on the driveway and on the road in front of my parents' house. I counted two cops, three firemen, and two guys in saggy coveralls who must have come with the ambulance. The whole group was milling and close to impatient. Elizabeth sat apart in a chair, with Mrs. Hodges standing uncomfortably near her side. When I entered the room my mother looked up at the neighbor and asked her, "now who is this now?"

"It's your son," Mrs. Hodges replied. "It's Danny. It's your son. He's here to take care of everything now."

"Where's Peter," Elizabeth asked her.

Mrs. Hodges looked at me beseechingly, as if I could make her understand that her husband, my father, was dead. The men in the room in their uniforms, more like rumpled work clothes, shifted uncomfortably. They were finished with their business here, I saw, and now just waiting for an appropriate moment to leave.

A cop recited to me their official account. It looked like an accidental drowning, he said. My father had swum out too far, miscalculated his strength, foundered before he could make it back to shore. He shouldn't have gone in alone, the officer said.

"He used to swim back there alone all the time," I said.

"We know that," he said. "Your neighbor here, Mrs. Hodges, she told us."

"He always took his time. He knew what he was doing. He was a good swimmer."

"But still," said the officer.

"Where is he now?"

"We have him in the ambulance now."

I asked if I could spend a moment alone with him. The men in the room shifted impatiently. They wanted to leave. But of course they couldn't refuse.

But alone in the back of the big boxy ambulance I didn't know what to do. It seemed impossible to say goodbye in there. The place was too barren, equipped with just gear. My father was inside a bag with a zipper. I had to at least look at him. I slipped open the zipper. He was still very wet. His chest was bare. I glanced around the hollow cabin and saw his clothing neatly folded and resting on a work counter, his shoes on the top of the stack. That would have been how he had left his things on the shore. Gathered as evidence, I guessed. I had wondered about the clothes, because I couldn't believe he could drown accidentally. If he had waded in while still fully dressed, I could have taken that fact as a sure sign of suicide, showing me for certain that he had meant to drown himself. The clothing would have been a drag that made swimming too hard. Especially the shoes. But he had stuck to his ritual and stripped down to his shorts. So how could I know that he hadn't just gone for a swim? How could he drown himself purposely? He was such an experienced swimmer, with such an effortless, leisurely stroke. It could take him for miles. Could he really just swim with the shore so near till he sank from exhaustion? Could he submerge and stay down till his lungs sucked in water? Even distraught and out of his mind, wouldn't he force himself back to the shallows, his body instinctively prodded by self-preservation?

Could he really feel desperate enough to overrule any impulse to survive? I just didn't know.

The loud metal latch on the ambulance door popped and the door sucked open like a refrigerator door. It was the cop from the livingroom.

"There's a few things I have to ask you," he said from outside, staying on the pavement and looking in through the wide opening. "It's for my report. You know, so I can write up my report. You live here, right? I mean, your neighbor, Mrs. Hodges, she wasn't sure. She says she sees you around here a lot, but she didn't want to say for sure that you live here."

"I don't really live here," I said. "I mean, I just came back here to stay. My wife and I just split up so I came here to stay. But it just happened."

"Happened when?"

"I came here on Sunday."

"Okay. So a couple of days ago. So, that was your stuff I saw in the room upstairs, in the bedroom? The suitcase and some boxes and stuff. That was your stuff up there?"

"Yeah, it's all mine."

"And you came here on Sunday? You moved in, we could say. Even though it's only been a few days, we could say you moved in here. For the last couple days this is the place you've been sleeping, the place you come home from work from and all that. We could say you live here, even if it's only been for a few days so far?"

"Yeah. For a few days I've lived here."

"Okay then, so there's one more thing I need to ask you. I need to know the last time you saw your father last night. So I can put it in my report."

"Last night?" I asked him.

"That's right. Last night."

I pushed my mind backward through the last twelve hours, through this morning before the phone call from Hodges, through my first moments at work, through the drive there, through waking in the house here this morning, my full night's sleep, arriving here yesterday evening after the scramble to find missing Trevor. I hadn't seen my father this morning and I hadn't seen him last night.

"Why last night?" I asked the officer.

"I just need to know the last time he was seen. Your mother, well, you know, she's not, you know, she's not reliable enough. I need to get an accurate report. You know: regulations."

"But why are you asking me about last night? Why aren't you asking me about this morning?"

"Because your father drowned last night."

Last night? I looked down at the face gaping out of the bag. Was it even my father, with its wan, bloodless lips and sunken dark eyes? But you always go swimming in the morning, I said silently to the corpse. What did you do?

"We'll know for sure after he's been, you know, after he's been examined," the policeman went on. "But from the way everything looks right now, the accident took place last night. Some time yesterday evening. Can you tell me when you saw him last?"

"I didn't see him yesterday."

"Not at all?"

"No. Not at all. Not in the evening, I mean. I saw him yesterday morning. Before I left for work."

"Was there anything, you know, different or unusual?"

"Different? Like what? What do you mean?"

"I don't know. I mean, did you notice any unusual behavior? Was there anything that upset him? Any phone calls or anything like that?"

Yesterday morning? Unusual? I pushed my mind back. It was barely more than twenty-four hours ago, yet suddenly yesterday morning seemed so far to reach back. What was he doing? I remembered: he was standing in the doorway of my bedroom, wringing and rocking and moaning because I had come there to stay. He had paced darkly through the house to tell me that my return there had tipped whatever uncertain balance he had managed to keep. He had spent that whole night sleepless and pacing and anxiously gnashing, or so I could easily guess.

I said to the policeman, "no, I didn't notice any unusual behavior."

"How come you only saw him in the morning? Why not the afternoon? Like, you know, when you got home from work yesterday? Isn't that kind of unusual? I mean, wouldn't you expect to see him when you got home from work? He was retired, right? Wouldn't you expect him to be here?"

"I got home late yesterday. I was out all day and half the night looking for someone."

"Looking for someone?"

"I was looking for a student. From the school. I work over there. I'm the psychologist. There was a problem with a student and I was out all day with his mother trying to find him. I can't go into details. It's all confidential. You know what I mean."

"But what time did you get home?"

"I don't know. I think it was about ten thirty. Maybe eleven."

"You were gone that long? Looking for a student? Did you

find him?"

"No."

"Did you report him missing?"

"No."

"Why not?"

"Under the circumstances I thought it would be better if his mother and I found him."

"But you didn't find him?"

"No."

"So he's still missing now?"

"No. I don't know. I guess so."

"And you still haven't reported it?"

"What does this have to do with my father?"

"I don't know. Nothing, I guess. As long as this boy's mother can confirm that you were with her till eleven last night. She can confirm that, can't she?"

"Of course she can."

"Who is the woman?"

"Her name is Linda Winkle."

"And you say your father was in bed when you got home?"

"I don't know. I thought he was. I didn't see him."

"Yeah. I figure you probably wouldn't have. We won't know for sure till after the, you know, after the examination. But if I had to guess, I would say he was already, you know, he was already deceased by then."

I closed my eyes.

"Look," said the cop, "I'm sorry I gotta go through all this right now. It's just that we couldn't really get much out of anybody else. You know, your mother and all. So anything you remember will really help put all the pieces together. What time did he normally go to bed?"

"I don't know what time he usually went to bed. I think it was different all the time, but I don't know for sure. I haven't been staying here that long. Remember? I've only been staying here for a couple of days."

"Right. You said that. Since when did you say, exactly?"

"Since Sunday. I moved back on Sunday. I just split up with my wife. I had to get out of the house. It's one of those things."

"Yeah. I know. One of those things. But just moving back here a couple of days ago, I'd say that's pretty unusual, wouldn't you? For your parents, I mean. I mean, that would be a pretty big change for you mother and father. Wouldn't you think?"

"I don't know. I guess so. Of course it would."

"But the only time you saw him was yesterday morning?"

"I saw him all the time because my mother was sick. I saw him on Sunday when I got here with all my boxes. Then I saw him yesterday morning before I went to work. Then I was out until late. Now this. Now I'll never see him again."

"Yeah. I know. I'm really sorry to put you through all these questions. It's just that, you know, there's regulations and everything. There's things I gotta put in my report."

The ambulance crew had come out of the house. The two men were milling impatiently behind the officer now. The fire lieutenant joined them. The three men stood behind the cop and looked in at me silently.

"There's one last thing," said the officer. "What about all the windows?"

"The windows?"

"Yeah. You know. How they're all busted out. Your neighbor, Mrs. Hodges, she told us your father did that."

"He's been under a lot of pressure lately. On account of my mother. He lost control of himself. About a week ago. Maybe two weeks ago. I was going to have them fixed. I just hadn't had time yet."

"He must of really had it rough," said the cop, shaking his head. "But he should of stayed out of that water alone."

By now the ambulance crew had climbed inside the van. The two men were working around me, tidying up for departure. I turned for a last look at my father. Long and gaunt, his body seemed insubstantial. I wanted to speak the word goodbye to him, to say it out loud so the word had a solid existence. But the two men around me were waiting now. The cop and the fireman outside were ready to leave. What did they usually hear in a case like this? Would goodbye be enough? The word wanted to spill from me. It wanted to fall, to clang like a steel span between my father and me. But would it sound insufficient? Or trite? A cliché? Insincere and just a show? In the end I stayed silent. I climbed out of the ambulance and left my father's body to their cold and mechanical care.

CHAPTER SEVENTEEN

Instead I impulsively trekked to the place where my father had spent the last instants of his life, as if his lingering imprint might remain faintly in the air there, or maybe in the water. Before starting on the trail toward the hidden pond, I stopped in the house to ask Mrs. Hodges to stay with my mother a little while longer. The neighbor was uncertain and quavering and clearly impatient to leave. But I knew that she would not refuse me.

The trail to the small lake began at a short, fallow field that touched the back border of my parents' yard. I knew the path well. As a boy growing up here I had walked on the trail every day. At least it had seemed like every day as I wandered toward quiet, secluded retreats that allowed me to linger and dream and to pass idle hours. But now the open plot behind the house was grown over with tall weeds and grasses intermixed with striving wild shrubs and aggressive young birch trees that pushed ever higher and closed around the old path. The trail scarcely remained open. It didn't look worn. I still knew the way, but it no longer seemed warmly familiar.

The same was true when I crossed the overgrown field and entered the patch of woods just beyond it. Beneath the trees here, relentlessly pioneering plants nearly hid the old path. No one ever walked here anymore. At least not until this morning. Or rather last night, when my father walked back to the pond. And here I was now, trodding the trail myself.

The land beneath the trees rose in a low ridge that kept the pond out of sight until I crested its top and began down the back side. From here the ground ran unbroken in a gentle downslope to the pool at its bottom. Through gaps between trees I peered metallic glints on the water that was now just a short walk downhill. I stretched my neck to see the patient lake more clearly, the lake where my father just died. Suddenly a body shot past me running full tilt toward the pond. It was Trevor.

I started after him. He was running very fast. Faster than I could run. I had to slow myself on the downslope unless I stumble and fall and splay headlong out of control. I looked down to keep my footing. When I glanced up I saw the sun glint sharply on the little lake that loomed like a chasm just ahead. Trevor was almost to the bank. I tried to run faster. By the time I reached the shore he had already flung off his shoes and his shirt and he was dashing into the water, pushing in past his knees and up over his thighs.

"What are you doing," I shouted at him.

"I'm going in," he yelled back.

"Going in where?"

"In the water."

"Why?"

"I don't know."

"You'd better come out."

"I can't."

"Why not?"

"I don't know."

"Come out."

"I'm gonna swim."

"What for?"

"For Peter."

"But Peter's not here. He's dead. He died this morning. Or last night. He died right here."

"I know."

"He drowned."

"I know."

"Then why are you going in?"

"I don't know."

"You'd better come out."

"I can't."

"Why not?"

"I don't know. I just want to go in."

Trevor pushed in farther. Suddenly he dropped down beneath the surface and sank full out of sight as he stepped past the shallows and fell into deep water. Just as abruptly his head popped up and bobbed on the water uncertainly like a loose grape. He flailed his arms awkwardly above the surface. The kid didn't know how to swim. Clearly he thought he knew how, judging from way he had rushed so recklessly into the lake. But he was just like so many other untrained youngsters who had never actually experienced the water. Who had never actually tried. He had only seen people swim, noticing how they appeared so effortless and adept when he watched them in television shows and movies, which led him to think that naturally he could swim also, as simply as he stood up from his bed in the morning and walked, an innate human trait he just had to possess. Or so he had blithely assumed. From the look of him, this was the first time he was actually attempting to swim himself. He arched his arms over his head in a desperate effort to pull himself forward. He kicked his legs furiously, churning a flurry of froth. He would tire himself fast. If he stayed in much longer he would drown himself for sure.

I pulled off my clothing and plunged in after him. Automatically my body braced for a chilling shock from cold water, but the pool felt unaccountably warm. I didn't wait to reach the drop-off but stretched into a crawl stroke where the water was only waist deep. My father had taught me to swim in this very pond. I pulled smoothly to Trevor in the span of only a few rapid strokes. I stopped beside him, keeping apart a safe distance. I stayed past his reach so he could not clutch me desperately and entangle us both. In his panic we both might drown.

"What do you think you're doing," I scolded the boy as I treaded the water. "Get back to shore now."

"I'm gonna go 'cross," he blew.

"What for?" But why was I even asking? I had to get Trevor out of the water. "Go back to shore," I commanded.

"I gotta make it 'cross," he sputtered

Trevor sucked in big, gulping breaths as he struggled to keep his head above water. He thrashed desperately, trying to swim. But he wasn't moving forward at all.

"Go back," I commanded.

With effort he stretched his head sideways to look at me. His expression looked pleading. Some panic flashed in his eyes.

"Kick your legs like scissors," I said. "Keep your arms

down. Keep them under the water. Wave them around under water but don't lift them up so high. Just keep waving them around under water. Keep kicking your legs. But kick them like scissors. Don't kick them so fast."

"I gotta go 'cross," he said stubbornly.

"No you don't."

"I gotta go 'cross for Peter."

"What for?"

"He'd want it."

"He wouldn't want you to drown."

"He'd want it," Trevor repeated

"I'll go across," I told him. "I'll go across for you. You go back to shore. Go back now."

I stayed in the spot treading water while he groped back toward shore in a tottering paddle. When he hit shallow water near the bank and began walking up to the beach, I stopped watching and spun away and slid horizontally into my stroke. I cut straight toward the pond's center, swimming fast to get across the water as quickly as I could. I would finish this just to keep the boy safely out of the lake. I pulled up once to check my progress. The far shore loomed near. It came fast. I swam into the shallows. I saw the bottom through the water just under me but I kept to my stroke until my knees scuffed the sand. I stood up and walked fully out of the pond. I walked onto the bank before I turned around to face the water again. I sat down on the shore. I crossed my arms on my up-bent knees and sank my head on my arms. I let my breaths come long and deep. My chest and shoulders lifted in heaves. My heart drubbed in echoing thuds. With my head low I watched loose water run off me in rivulets that merged to larger veins on the ground and ran down the low slope to rejoin the lake. The sun felt warming on my shoulders and back. I could swim here more often if I wanted. I sat alone. I gazed across the pond at Trevor waiting on the other shore. He was standing, pacing, glancing toward me, twitching away, holding his gaze in the far direction, looking up the ridge toward the house as if the treetops there held vital importance. He appeared far off and small. The still pond between us now seemed unaccountably large. Isolation descended on me in a moaning arrival. I sat alone in the puddle my own drips had made. My father was dead and my mother was lost and my wife had abandoned me. No one was left.

I stood up quickly and waded back into the pond. I plunged in without any dread of cool water and I stretched to an overhand crawl, my body flat in a racer's posture, my face down and rotating sideways for breaths. I swam fast. I felt the bite of my limbs through the water. I felt my body glide as its exertions pulled me deeper into the pool. I felt the striving rotations of my arms and I felt my scissor kicks slice in singing rhythm. I felt the sun's warmth on my shoulders skimming the surface. I tasted the sweet, laden, brimming freshness of the living pool. The water encased me.

But I should have rested longer on the far bank before I had started back. Somewhere near the center of the pond my shoulders panged and started tiring. My hips, buttocks and thighs gelled and tingled from the incessant kicking. Resistance from the water remained unrelenting. The pool locked around me. Instinctively I pulled up from my rapid racer's stroke. I drew in deep breaths. I rolled to my back and spread my arms for buoyancy. I spread my legs in a vee. I closed my legs. I opened them to a vee. I pulsed them together again slowly, leisurely, closing my legs and opening them and closing them to create the forward thrust my body needed to keep above water. Gliding on my back I clapped my outspread arms to my sides and opened them again and pushed them again to my sides to cause more thrust to help keep my body gently moving. I rested while leisurely I worked my arms and my legs.

When forward travel stops, a swimmer sinks. But no rule says the forward movement must be fast. Trevor's vertical thrashing would have sunk him, pulled him down by his plumb posture. But Peter, my father, could loll forever on the water with his easygoing breast stroke. Likewise on my back, as I now rested. I pushed myself with the effortless pulses of a jelly fish. I spread my legs in a vee and closed them, spread them and closed them, spread them and closed them leisurely. I opened my arms and clapped them slowly back along my sides, open and back, open and back, leisurely resting on my back in an easy stroke. I raised my head to watch the water slowly recede behind me as I glided. I saw the small wake my body made as I pushed through the pool. Small ripples from my kicks and my pulsing arms spread behind me in a widening wedge that grew faint on the surface and soon disappeared behind me, leaving the water where I had passed perfectly level and flat and indifferent. The pond could swallow me and have not a care. I could never permanently mark it.

I rolled from my back and laid prone, face down in the water again. I lifted my head to see the far shore. Trevor still waited. He was pacing still, uncertain. He was looking at me now, though he gazed away once again when he saw me lift my head to see him. He peered into the treetops some more. Yet he watched me. Maybe he thought I was tired still. Maybe he wondered if I could swim the full distance back to shore. If I stayed out much longer he might plunge in again, I said to myself. It was time to swim back, I thought. I would just have to swim back more slowly. With my head above the surface I pushed my arms ahead of me and stroked them back horizontally, in plane with the water. I kicked my legs the same way, not piercing the surface but thrusting like a closing vee. Floating on my chest, I held my head above the surface, forward facing, my limbs pushing me almost with minimal effort. This was my father's breast stroke, flat like a frog except for my head that stuck out vertically over the water. I had never swum it before. I could loll forever on the water with this easygoing stroke.

When I reached the shore Trevor stepped to the water's edge as I climbed out.

"Where did you come from," I asked him.

"I've been waiting right here like you told me."

"No. I mean before. How did you get here this morning?"

"I was in the garage."

"The garage? What were you doing in there?"

"I was in there all night."

"In the garage?"

"I slept there."

"You mean you came here when you took off yesterday? You were here last night? You were right here all along? Right under my nose? What time did you get here?"

"I don't know what time it was when I got here."

"Did you come here right away?"

"Pretty much. It took me a while to get rides. I hitchhiked here," he announced a little triumphantly.

"I guess I should have listened to the kids," I said.

"What kids?"

"At school. I asked some of them which way you'd gone when you left yesterday and they said you turned left at the end of the parking lot. I was sure you would have gone the other way. I should have listened to them. I just never thought you might come here."

"I couldn't think of any place else to go."

"Your mother and I spent the whole day looking for you."

"I know. I heard you telling the cop."

"It should have occurred to me to look here. I can't believe I never thought of it."

"Where is she now?"

"I don't know. Not exactly. I think she left for Florida already."

"Yeah. I figured that." He dropped his head as he said it.

Whiffing his dejection, instinctively I lied to counteract it.

"But she spent the whole day looking for you," I said. "I was with her. She didn't want to leave until she found you. We looked everywhere. I guess it just got to the point where she couldn't wait any longer."

"So what. What difference does it make." He gazed away. His eyes darkened. He grew more bewildered. He looked battered, betrayed, resigned and defeated. But he was still only fourteen years old.

"But she really wanted to find you," I said to him.

"What for? She was just gonna leave me here anyway."

"No she wasn't."

"Yes she was."

"No, she wasn't."

"She wasn't?"

"No."

"Yes she was. That's what she told me."

"Maybe she was at first, but then she changed her mind. She said she was going to take you. That's why we spent the whole day out searching for you. She made me drive her. I didn't want to but she made me. But then when we couldn't find you, well, I guess she just had to get going. She had a tight schedule to keep and everything."

"Really?"

"Yeah."

"Did she tell you that?"

"Of course she did. Why do you think we spent the whole day out looking for you? Did you see what time it was when I got home last night?"

"It was pretty late."

"Well, that's where I'd been."

"Yeah. I heard you explaining all that to the cop."

"Before she left we worked it out so that you can stay here for a while."

"Really?"

"Yeah. I have to work out some details, but I think we can get everything arranged, especially if you agree to it and everything."

"Oh, I agree to it. Sure."

"Good," I said. "Now we better get back to the house. I left my mother there with Mrs. Hodges. She's a neighbor here. I shouldn't keep her waiting much longer."

But Trevor lingered, gazing into the pool, scanning around the bank as if something had fallen, as if a wallet or keys or a comb had dropped out of his pocket and he wanted to pick it up before we walked back.

"I've never known anybody who's died before," he said after a pause. "Is the ambulance gone now?"

"Yeah. It's gone."

"At least you got to see him before they left. Did you say good-bye to him?"

"Yeah. I said good-bye."

"I was hiding in the garage but then I saw you start to walk back here. I figured this is where you'd be going. After all that I saw this morning – I mean, I was here when everything happened. When the ambulance got here. The cops and the firemen. I was hiding when it all happened. I could figure it out from what they were saying. I saw them bring Peter from back this way. When I saw you start to walk back here I figured this is where you were going. I wanted to come back here too. That's when I left the garage. I snuck out 'cause I wasn't sure if anyone was here still. I took off so no one would stop me. That's why I ran past you so fast. I didn't want you to stop me. Then I just ran in the water. I just ran in automatically. Who knows why. I just ran in. I was going to go all the way across. I'm glad you did it. I'm glad you went all the way across."

"You've got to be careful," I said to him gravely. "Water is dangerous. Even my father . . . and he was an experienced swimmer."

"How could he drown?" Trevor asked me.

"I don't know."

"I heard what you said. I heard you tell the cop he was such a good swimmer."

"He was."

"Then how could he drown?"

"I don't know how he drowned. I'm not so sure that he did."

"He did. They said he did. I heard all the cops say it before you even got here."

"I know," I said. "That's not what I meant. I just mean I don't know if he drowned accidentally. I don't know if it was an accident."

"What else could it be?" Trevor asked me.

"I don't know," I said.

"You mean, like, it was suicide or something?"

"I don't know."

"Peter wouldn't do that."

"I don't know what he'd do anymore."

"How come you stopped in the middle out there?" Trevor asked me.

"I got tired," I said. "I was just swimming back and then I got tired."

"You see. Even you got tired," he said. "It's a long way to swim. You're a good swimmer too. I could see that. You're a good swimmer just like your father. But you got tired going across. It's just a long way to swim."

"But my father swam over and back every day. At least in the summer. At least he used to. Right up to this year. He used to swim over and back as a morning routine. All the way. He knew exactly how far it was and he knew how to swim it."

"But not this year. You just said that. Was this the first time he came back here this year?"

"I don't know. It might have been. He told me he wasn't swimming anymore because he couldn't leave my mom alone long enough. But I don't know."

"So maybe he just didn't know," Trevor said. "He was just out of shape," he insisted. "That's what it was. He was just out of shape and he just didn't know. He just shouldn't of gone in the water alone. Like that cop said. He just shouldn't of gone in alone."

"But he knew this. He did it every day. You don't forget. He knew what to expect."

"But not this year."

"Why did he come back here now," I wondered. "Usually he would have been swimming back here for more than a month now. But not this year. He'd given it up. That's what he told me and from all that I saw I believe him. So why did he come back here now? Why did he pick this morning to swim?"

"Last night," Trevor corrected. "It happened last night."

"That's even stranger," I said. "He never came back here at night. He always just swam in the mornings."

"Do you think it was dark?"

"I don't know. Maybe. They didn't give me a time."

"That's what it was," Trevor said. "It had to be dark. Things are always different when it's dark."

"But why would he come back here then? He never came back here to swim at night. Why now? Unless he wanted to . . .." My voice trailed to silence.

"I guess he just wanted to swim," Trevor said quietly, the words spoken more to himself. "He just wanted to swim. He just shouldn't of done it alone. Like the cop said. He shouldn't of done it alone."

I looked at the boy. He stared steadfastly into the pool. Silent. At depth.

"You just always have to be careful," I said. "It's a lesson. When you went in just now, I could see you're in trouble. You always have to be careful."

"I know. I just needed to go in the water."

"You'd better let me teach you how to swim first."

"Really? Can you do that?"

"I think so."

CHAPTER EIGHTEEN

I regretted taking in the boy almost immediately. I just didn't know what to do with him. I should have known. After all, psycho-coaching children was my job. But caring for a child for just an hour in a far-away office is fathoms shallower than caring for a child always, in your home. It was so much easier, so superficial, to counsel child after child after child for half-hour sessions through eight-to-five work days, than it was to care for only one around the clock, owning the responsibility entirely. Owning it to the full depth of enervating concern and affection. Owning the worry. Owning the frustration. Owning the doubts. Owning expectations and their wedded disappointments. Owning all the hidden intimacies of home life, the chewing and crumbs, the sleep sounds, the sooty fingers, the table grunts, bathroom odors, scratchings, gurgles, farts, the oily hair, pores, curled toes, pimples and all of the other organic gaffs silently endured and unmentioned.

Handling the authorities was much easier – an irony, because instead of the chafing at home, I had expected all the friction to come from the state's kinder-care agents, with their tangled rules and stiff barricades of paperwork. But Tweed helped me beat the bureaucrats, using her connections at all the appropriate agencies, and no doubt calling in some favors as well, to secure my state-sanctioned guardianship of Trevor Winkle. Through my open office door I listened to her exercise her telephone to do it. She was officious, chatty, off-the-point and superficially personal, concealing her fervid self-interest. Through conversations she maneuvered with crafty precision person-to-person among the clerks, secretaries, and untitled assistants who push the papers that retain real authority. As long as a thing is written on a form, it is valid to government workers. Tweed toiled with intensity, completing one telephone call and immediately dialing the next. She seemed tireless. I would have felt flattered to think she was toiling so hard just for me, as a favor, perhaps, or maybe an act of friendship. But I knew better. Vivian Tweed was pushed by revenge. She saw the task as a means to punish Trevor's mother, her rival, Linda Winkle. Rather than any big-hearted impulse to assist either me or the boy, she merely wanted to take Linda's son away from her, the same as Linda had stolen Tweed's Alfred from her. That motive was plain from the relish Tweed showed as she worked her pliant telephone. Still, I felt grateful to her for cutting through so much administrative muck for me.

But then I was stuck. School was out till September. Summer was already settling into its long stretch of ordinary days. Trevor was only fourteen. My mother was only a presence, walking, sleeping, eating, talking, but wholly disconnected by a scrambled mind slowly sucked away by age. The whole household rested on me.

I had to start feeding us. By the time we got through the guardianship signing, the closeout of school, and my father's dolorous funeral, the cupboards in my parents' worn house had run bare. The refrigerator was stripped empty. Even all the breakfast cereal was eaten. I drove to the grocery store cradling the notion that I needed to buy foods for the types of meals I had always associated with the house, the meals my mom had made, legitimate meals built from scratch ingredients. After all, a home creases rituals into its people. I bought whole potatoes, fresh greens for salads, carrots, celery, cukes and red tomatoes. I bought a whole chicken for soup. Beef shaded burgundy-rose. Grapes from Peru that popped between teeth. Two bars of a crumbly cheddar. Crackers, of course. One dozen eggs. A loop of smoked sausage. Tart pickles. A tin of olive oil. Bottled cranberry juice. A five-pound bag of flour. Sugar in a paper sack. I filled the shopping cart until it got tough to push from its weight and inertia.

When I returned home Trevor was in the back yard with the mower. Now that was surprising. I had told him to stay inside the house with Elizabeth. I had reminded him earnestly when I left for the store that he could not leave her alone, that if unwatched she might pull on her shoes and silently step out of the house and wander down streets and get lost. Or maybe stray to the basement and toggle some switch, lever or button that fouled up some operation or some appliance that we needed up in the house. Or perhaps tread upstairs and pull boxes from closets and scatter possessions that I would only have to collect and put back. Yet here he was, outside mowing the grass. I hustled into the house where Trevor had left her. I found my mother asleep in the living room, slumped and curled on a spongy chair, her mouth hinged open. Trevor had done all right after all. We both understood she would stay like that for an hour or more. I watched him for a moment through the window, bent behind the mower, walking at an earnest gait, pushing with full concentration. He liked to keep at the grass, to keep it cut, well trimmed and orderly. As I watched him, the mad neighbor Watts suddenly appeared beyond Trevor, emerging hastily from his own garage with a chainsaw and pulling the chord frantically to start it so that he could make some droning noise too. Who knew what limb or log he was cutting? Who cared? Trevor kept at his task, unnoticing, pacing placidly behind the whirring mower. I turned away. Ignoring insistent old Watts was effortless in the background of the boy.

I stepped outside again to fetch all the lumpy, sagging grocery bags from the car. As I unpacked them in the kitchen, the refrigerator and cupboards seemed grateful. I took care to load them with orderly precision, arranging boxes and bags, cans, containers and clumps of fresh foods for easy selection when later I would pull out ingredients to make a meal. But when? Or, more fundamentally, what? With the shopping all done and the foods patly waiting, I sat down at the table in the kitchen and looked all around me. I had no idea how to make the meals I had pictured steaming in front of the three of us.

Trevor came in for a break. He filled a glass at the tap and drank it down completely while he stood at the sink. He refilled the glass and brought it to the table where I sat, settling into a chair himself for a breath and a pause and a moment of quiet.

Elizabeth pattered in right after him, as if she'd been waiting. I had not even heard her wake up. She carried a bucket that splashed over with sudsy water. She announced that she needed to clean the floor beneath the refrigerator.

"Danny, will you pull it out from the wall for me," she asked.

Trevor stood up at once, though he stayed to take a swallow of water before he stepped to the fridge. He spread his feet and lowered his back and clamped his arms around the sides of the big appliance. He nudged it away from the wall and then slipped behind it to pull the electrical cord from the outlet. While Trevor settled back into his chair at the table, Elizabeth wedged herself behind the refrigerator. Awkwardly she sank to the floor, letting the bucket thud down hard so that water with suds spilled over the top. She pulled a tattered gray rag from the pail and swabbed in clumsy arcs around herself.

"I should have cleaned back here a long time ago," she said. She stopped and stretched up her spine and wiped the back of her forearm against her brow.

"Danny," she called, "can you to pull the icebox out a little bit more?"

Trevor stood up again and wiggled the refrigerator back another few inches.

"I need more room back here to scrub," Elizabeth said.

"Is that okay now," Trevor asked her.

"I think so," she said. "How do you suppose it got so dirty back here?"

"I don't know. I guess that's just where all the dirt goes."

"Oh, sure it does," said Elizabeth. "But don't you think we should have cleaned back here before now?"

"No one ever looks under there," Trevor said.

"But I should have been back here long before this. It's not right to let it go for so long. It gets so dirty. Could you pull it out just a little more, Dan. I need a little more room still."

Trevor edged the refrigerator a tad further away from the wall.

"How's that," he asked.

"That should do just perfectly."

Elizabeth bent to it again, attacking the grime earnestly but completely ineffectually. Then unaccountably she stopped. She straightened her back again. She wiped her forehead with the back of her arm. She stood up and walked away. She left the room. Only an echo of silence remained, with the pail of soapy water abandoned on the linoleum behind the refrigerator and the shred of a rag heaped beside it. It was clear that she wouldn't be back.

Trevor walked over and picked up the rag and wiped away a dollop of suds that had sloshed on the floor from the bucket. He carried the pail to the sink. He emptied it. He rinsed it thoroughly with clear water from the tap. He perched the pail upside-down on the dripboard beside the sink to drain. He wrung water from the rag and soaked it again with clear water from the tap and wrung it hard a second time. He opened the rag and draped it over the faucet to dry. He nudged the refrigerator back into its recess next to the wall before he returned to the table and swallowed a long drink from his glassful of water.

He spun the glass idly on the table for a moment. He looked at his fingertips. He held them to his nose and sniffed them and said, "I've been noticing this smell in the corner back there where I'm cutting the grass. When I cut into the weeds at the edge way back there. It smells really strong. But its nice. I like it. I just don't know what it is. I never smelled anything like it before. I have no idea what it is. It must be some kind of weed or something. I picked a leave and rubbed it on my fingers so I could keep smelling it. I love that smell." He reached his fingers toward my nose for me to sample. For an instant I balked at the intimacy, but then I corrected myself and sniffed.

"That's basil," I said. "That's growing out there? Really?"

"It's growing all over the place. It must be wild."

"It's not wild," I told him. "My mother, Elizabeth, she used to have a garden back there. She grew all sorts of stuff. She always said basil was her favorite. She liked it a lot too."

"So she's still growing it?"

"No. It must be self-sowing. It's coming up on its own every year. From seeds the plants drop. I had no idea it was still growing back there."

"What do you do with it?"

"You cook with it."

"You eat it?"

"Well, yeah. But not like in a salad or anything like that. It's not like lettuce or spinach or something. It's a flavoring. You use it in foods. Like a spice."

"What kinds of foods?"

"I don't know. Italian food, I guess. Italians use it a lot. They make something called pesto. Other things too, I guess. I never really cooked much with it. I never really cooked much at all."

"What did Elizabeth make with it?"

"I don't know what she made," I answered. "I just remember it being here."

"Do you think she can tell you?"

"I don't think so." But I looked across at the low, cluttered shelf that held my mother's cooking books. There, just visible beneath a stack of what looked to be utility bills and a discarded candy wrapper too I saw the dinged and spattered recipe box my mother once had kept. I stepped to the shelf and dug out the box and carried it back to the table.

"She kept all her best recipes in here," I said to Trevor. "I really don't know what she did with the basil. The meals were always just here and I never really paid any attention to how she made them or what she put in them. They were good meals, for sure, but I never paid any attention to how she made them."

"But she saved her recipes?"

"Yeah."

"In here?"

"She kept her favorite ones in here. Yeah."

"Then all you got to do is read the recipes. Right?"

"Well, right. I guess so."

Trevor drained away the last swallow of water from his glass. He wiped his lips with the back of his hand. He raised his fingers delicately to his nose and inhaled the sweet aroma of the herb. Abruptly he rose. He placed the empty glass inside the sink as he passed it.

"I guess I better get back out there," he said. "There's still a lot of grass to cut."

"Are there any tall plants still back there," I called before he got out the door.

"What?"

"The basil. Are there any tall basil plants still growing, or did you mow it all down?"

"There's some tall ones, yeah. Back by the edge of the grass, where the field starts. There's some tall ones back in there where I didn't mow."

"Can you pick some for me?"

"Pick some?"

"Yes pick some. I'll try to make something with it. Pick a big handful of the leaves and bring them in to me. I'll see if I can find a recipe in here that uses it."

"Really?"

"Yes really. Just get me some. Go get it now."

Trevor went out. He didn't seem shaken by my outburst, but still I felt sorry for snapping at him. I was anxious and unsettled by the thought that I had to cook now. And now I'd use basil. Was all that I needed really right here in this battered old recipe box? Expecting salvation inside, I lifted the lid. If I was going to care for my ailing old mom and this dispossessed boy, the best way to start was with one good meal.

ABOUT THE AUTHOR

Jeffrey Zygmont writes stories about free people who possess rebellious impulses. His books tell about independent characters in conflict with collected groups and their constraining beliefs. In addition to *The Dropout*, that theme of defiant independence animates two other current novels: *I Am Bill Gates' Dog*, and *Ad Man in the Games of 2046*.

Jeffrey Zygmont's short fiction has appeared in the anthology The Literature of Work, and in periodicals ranging from *New Hampshire Journal* to the magazine *Twin Cities Business Monthly*. His poetry has appeared in the journal *Not Just Air*. Two of his poems received nominations for the annual Pushcart Prize, a respected literary award. They are "Wife Poem XXVII," nominated in 2008, and "Menopause," nominated in 2009. Zygmont's novel *The Dropout* was the July 2002 Featured Selection of the pioneering ebook publisher Online Originals.

As a journalist, Zygmont has published articles in magazines and newspapers including *Boston Magazine, Boston Woman, Business Week, CFO Magazine, The Christian Science Monitor, Cigar Aficionado, Gannett Newspapers, Inc Magazine, The Boston Globe Sunday Magazine,* and *Robb Report*. He was the automobile columnist for *Omni Magazine*, a technology columnist for *PC Computing Magazine*, and an editor for *High Technology Magazine*. His non-fiction books are *Microchip; An Idea, Its Genesis and the Revolution It Created*, and *The VC Way; Investment Secrets from the Wizards of Venture Capital*, which was translated into Chinese for sale in that country.

www.ingramcontent.com/pod-product-compliance
Lightning Source LLC
Chambersburg PA
CBHW050031180626
46810CB00002B/673